GRACE ANNE

THE WAITE FAMILY SERIES

BOOK 6

KATHI S. BARTON

World Castle Publishing, LLC
Pensacola, Florida
Copyright © Kathi S. Barton 2013
Print ISBN: 9781939865090
eBook ISBN: 9781939865106
First Edition World Castle Publishing, LLC March 10, 2013
http://www.worldcastlepublishing.com
Licensing Notes
Cover: Karen Fuller
Photos: Shutterstock
Editor: Brieanna Robertson

Chapter 1

Michael Cunningham parked his car in the lot and scowled at the building. He didn't have time for this shit and he didn't want to meet up with the owner of this building to settle something that should have been settled over three months ago. He pulled out his cell phone when it rang and answered with a bark of his name.

"I'm wondering if you ever look at your caller ID before you answer, or is it just me that gets such special treatment? I mean, if it helps, I will ground you until you see your way to be nice to your mother." He heard her laugh as she continued. "Of course, I suppose I shouldn't expect anything less of the man who fired his own brother this morning."

"He came running to you, did he? I don't know what he expected me to do. He was having...he was doing something on company time that got him into trouble this time. And don't even ask me to hire him back. I won't do it, not this time."

Michael had stepped off the elevator this morning to see his brother Thomas fucking his secretary on her desk. And if that wasn't bad enough, his brother had asked him if he wanted sloppy seconds when he was finished. He wasn't going to tell his mom that, but he was reasonably sure she already knew.

"No," she said with a heavy sigh. "I don't want you to hire him back. You've done all you can for the idiot. Melody is probably

5

going to file some sort of charges against us. I'm sure there is some rule about being fucked by your boss on your own desk."

Michael winced. "There is, but I don't think she's going to have much to use." He took a breath before telling her the best part. "She told me that she was banging the guy in accounting too and one more on her list was fine by her."

"Oh good heavens. Where do we get these people? I swear to you... Where are you now? That new man...Donald, said you'd left the site."

He looked up at the building again. "I'm at the Washington building again. The last time I was here they told me the owner was out of town. They wouldn't even tell me when he was coming back. I couldn't even get the man who was prancing around taking pictures to tell me."

"Prancing? Michael, do we need to send you to those sensitive classes again? Men do not prance." She laughed again and he smiled. He loved his mom.

"Okay, not prancing, but he was having too much fun for me to believe he was working. What the hell are they supposed to be doing in there anyway? All we could find out were designs. Designs of what, is what I'd like to know." He picked up the file on his passenger seat. "Some person by the name of G. A. Waite and he bought the building back ten years ago for a song. I want it and he'll sell it to me or I'll put him and his happy little workers out of business."

He got out of his car and straightened his tie as his mother reminded him about the meeting he had at a luncheon. He didn't give two figs for the meeting right now as he mentally assessed the building and the grounds surrounding it. He put his phone away and simply walked inside the door. The place was never locked up, as far as he knew, and he didn't have any problems this time.

The place was in shambles. He supposed it wasn't really as bad as he first thought, but a sort of chaotic mess. He hated things not in their place and this one, this large building, was a nightmare to him. The colors alone were enough to make a grown man sick—pinks and greens mixed with heavy doses of blue and black. There was an

6

entire wall of prints that had no business being together no matter what the idea had been to paste them all together. He looked up when someone came toward him.

"You're over an hour late. And what is that supposed to be you're wearing?"

Michael looked down at his suit and tie.

"It'll have to go. And that tie. Oh. My. God. Who dressed you? Your mother?"

Before he could make a comment on the clothes the woman had on, she was pulling him along behind her by his tie. He nearly stopped and made her explain. He nearly did, as a matter of fact, but he was suddenly speechless and his tongue had stuck to the roof of his mouth. Holy good Christ, he was in a porn movie.

There were perhaps five or six half dressed men and women everywhere; some of them were even wearing some sort of sparkles on their body and in their hair. And the bed...hell, is was big enough for all of them.

~~~

Gracie stood frowning at her assistant again. "I still don't see why I have to model this. I hired you to find people to do this sort of thing. Besides, I have things to do this morning and it doesn't involve me standing in front of a camera for eight hours straight."

Becky snorted. "You probably look better in it than that stupid cow Marcie could ever hope to. So unless you have a hot date with a *real* person and not a toy, forget it. We need this shot today for the cover and you're the one who designed it."

Gracie wanted to point out that she was the boss and that she had designed all the outfits on all the covers and inside, but she bit her lip. Becky was right, the magazine had to be completed today or they'd be late in getting the Christmas catalogue out. She glanced over at the calendar. It was only May and she was worrying about a catalogue that was still five months from being sent out.

Looking in the mirror, she thought the design was simply beautiful. She turned to her right then left, looking at the way the color of the bra and panty set complemented her skin color. The pale of her skin against the dark blue of the material was better than

7

she'd hoped for. Unless, of course, she remembered that she wasn't supposed to be the model, but the one behind the camera directing the shoot. She tried again to get someone else to do it and, of course, she was ignored. She wondered, not for the first time, when she'd lost control here. She smiled, knowing that she'd never really had it.

"The model we hired just showed up finally. And for the record, I told them to send him over in a t-shirt and jeans. Not that he doesn't look scrumptious like he is, but I did tell them." Margo picked up one of the other outfits that needed to be re-shot. "You know, if I weren't in a semi-serious failing relationship, I'd have to try and get some of what that guy is hiding under that cool, 'don't fucking touch me' look. I mussed his tie just to see what he'd do."

"He has on a tie? A suit…" Gracie looked at her assistant. "Tell him to lose the jacket if he has one and to roll up his sleeves. Leave the tie…wait." Everyone froze. "What color is the tie?"

By the time she had the idea in her head nothing else mattered. She pulled her robe on and walked into the set. Christ, love a dub, he was scrumptious. And he looked pissed. She walked over to him and eyed him critically. Yes, she knew he was going to be perfect.

"Would you mind telling me why this…person is telling me I have to remove my jacket? I assure you that—"

"Don't talk or I'll make sure you're not paid." She fingered the tie and then looked up at him. "I really think you need to take off the jacket. I'm already behind schedule and you coming here late has put me more behind." She wasn't sure he was going to comply, not with the look of murder in his eye. "Now would be a good time to be a good boy and take the fucking jacket off."

"And if I do, what do you take off?"

She heard the tone. And she hated that her body reacted to it. When he started to unbutton his jacket and then remove it she couldn't seem to catch her breath. When he laughed, she looked up at his face. "You think this is fun? Well, it's not. I have ten hours to get this shot right and I won't put up with your being snarky. This is a photo shoot where I'm the boss and you're going to do as you're told. Roll up the sleeves and do what I tell you or you'll never work here again."

She knew it was a good threat under normal circumstances, but this guy could probably get a job anywhere no matter what he did to fuck up this one. He was just too good-looking, and sexy as hell. She stood there until he rolled first the left, then the right sleeve up without taking his eyes from her face. She never blinked an eye when she unbelted her robe.

"Gracie, there's a call for you. It's that ditzy sister...the one...fuck, what's her name? She wants to tell you something," Becky said from across the room. "Jazzie, the author. That's it."

"Tell her I'll call her back tonight. Unless it's a matter of life or death." Becky said that it wasn't and that she could call Jazzie tonight.

She heard his breath catch when she tossed off the robe. She stood before him in her panties and bra, if that was what you could call a tiny scrap of lace over her nipples and less over her mound. And it was almost an exact match to his tie. She stepped toward him and he reached for her. She put her hand up to stop him.

"You aren't in charge here, big boy. See the camera over there? That's Arnold Malone holding it up. Arnold is going to shoot more pictures than I can count and you're going to stand here like a good model and let him. Understand?"

"Model? I'm not—"

"Okay, so you're something else. Whatever. Stand there and put your hands where he or I tells you and shut up. Get it?"

He glared, but nodded.

"Good. See the mock ups over there against the wall?"

Again, he nodded.

"That's what I need to redo. The one where we're supposed to be turned on by what I'm wearing." She turned her back to him and waited until he put his hand on her belly just above the panties line and his other hand wrapped around her neck and pulled her back. The moment he touched her she knew this wasn't going to work. Before she could pull away he tightened his arms around her.

"Easy, princess. This is supposed to be a sensual shot, remember? Relax." His mouth brushed over the column of her neck

9

before he nipped at her skin. "You taste like warm sunshine and smell like an apple pie."

"You're not supposed to do that," she told him breathlessly. "You're supposed to be…" She lost her train of thought when he ran his tongue along her spine. "We aren't making a porn movie."

"Hummm," he hummed as he nipped her again. "Maybe we should be. A woman like you, soft and warm, should be making lots of money doing stuff like this."

She tried to think. And some part of her mind registered that Arnold was saying something, though for the life of her she couldn't understand what. When her model turned her in his arms, spread his hand over her lower back, and his little finger nudged under the elastic of the panties, she took his tie and yanked his mouth to hers.

The kiss should have been chaste. It should have been a brushing of mouths together. It should have meant nothing. But holy moly, this man could kiss. His tongue speared deep into her mouth and slid along her own. He was hot, heavenly, and oh so delicious. She wrapped the tie tighter in her hand and held on, no longer concerned with the shot, but being consumed by this man. When he lifted her leg and wrapped it over his hip, she moaned and pressed into him. His deep growl had her pussy flood with desire and need. When he broke off the kiss, she whimpered.

"We're not alone. And I have to meet someone," he told her as he bit her earlobe. "Tell me where I can find G. A. Waite and I can finish up with him and we can take up where we left off."

"G. A?" She felt disorientated and dizzy. That's when she started to hear the things around her. "I don't…why?"

With another quick nip to her mouth he rocked into. "Because I want to fuck you. But I need to get this Waite person to sell me his fucking building first."

She took a step back, then another. She was reaching for the robe that Becky was holding out for her when she realized who he was. "Michael Cunningham of Cunningham and Cunningham, I presume?"

"Yes." He looked around the room before looking back at her. "And you would be?"

"Grace Anne Waite of G. A. Waite, as in Gracie Anne Designs. And I told you before, Mr. Cunningham, I'm not selling my building." She looked over at the people who seemed to have been frozen in place. "Get him out of my building and burn the shots. We won't be able to use them. I'm sure he'll sue just to get what he wants."

"Now, see here. I need this—"

"I don't give a good fuck what you need. Get out." She turned her back to him and started toward her office. She'd been humiliated and hurt, but there was no way in hell she'd let him see it.

"This isn't finished, Miss. Waite. I get what I want and your little design business isn't going to stand in my way," he shouted as Mark ushered him to the door. He continued to shout at her then there was silence.

Michael Cunningham was her worst nightmare and the sexiest man she'd ever seen, and tasted for that matter. She stepped behind the curtain to change back into her street clothes when she heard her door open.

"Go away," she told whoever it was. "I'm not going to come out until you leave the room."

"Good, then you can't get away. Want to tell me why I have to burn the best pictures I've ever shot and the best ones to come out of this building since…well, since forever?"

She closed her eyes and wanted to scream at her friend Arnold to let it go. But she knew him well enough to know that he'd stay there until she gave in or the next issue was due. She pulled her shirt over her head and stepped out. He was sitting on the small loveseat. She glared at him as he held up his camera.

"They can't possibly be the best pictures you've ever taken. You're much too professional to use what could only amount to pornography pictures taken in less than five minutes." She sat at her desk and pulled the first thing she could reach to her. Unfortunately, it was the front cover mockup of the catalogue they were shooting.

"It was twenty minutes and they aren't porn. They are going to sell you more underwear than anything else you come up with.

11

Christ, the room was practically on fire with you two. I've never seen you react that way..." He stopped talking when she glared.

"Forget it. He'll never let us use them no matter how good they are, and—"

He cut her off when he stood up and came to her desk with his computer. "They aren't good, Gracie, they're magnificent. Let me show you." She sat back and let him set up on her desk. "I thought at first I'd get some shots to tease you with. I thought the man was just too pretty and, yeah, too handsome to do anything more than sell him instead of your clothing line. Then he touched you and you...well, look. He's looking at you like he wants to have you for Christmas dinner and then maybe a little bit into the New Year too."

There were perhaps sixty pictures on his screen. They were too small for her to make out what they were like this, so he clicked on the first one and it blew up to full screen. She was standing in front of Cunningham and they were looking at each other like sworn enemies rather than what Arnold had said. Before she could comment, he started talking again.

"I knew there was going to be chemistry, I just didn't know what sort. As you can see, the two of you look like kids in a play yard ready to throw down the gauntlet." He clicked ahead a few more pictures to one where he is licking her neck. "Then he got into it. Or better yet, he got into you. Christ, look at that face. You look sexy and wanton. Like you could let him take you right then and there."

She flushed knowing that she had wanted him to. She had wanted Michael so badly that she'd forgotten that they were in a room full of people, full of her employees, and that this man was trying to kick her out of the building she'd worked very hard to get.

"It doesn't matter. He's a dead end. Call the agency tomorrow and get someone else. And that guy that was supposed to be here today, never use him again and put the word out. I don't want him fucking up another shoot."

Arnold left her office and she sat there for several minutes thinking about what had just happened. She had been staring at the note on her desk to call her sister for a few minutes more when she picked up the phone. Jazzie answered on the first ring.

"I'm going to have a baby," she screamed in the phone when she answered.

Chapter 2

Michael didn't get a damned thing done because of the woman. He didn't even try and justify that he was thinking about the building; it was her. Grace Anne, she'd said her name was. And it suited her.

He thought of the way she'd fit against his body. The way her mouth felt under his. He reached down and adjusted his cock for what he was sure was the millionth time since yesterday. She had even haunted his dreams. He glared at the report on his desk again. And that was not helping one bit.

He picked it up just as his phone rang. He tossed it down with a snarl and answered with a bark of his name. Thankfully, his secretary was used to his moods of late and didn't make a comment about it.

"There is a gentleman here to see you, sir, a Mr. Arnold Malone. He said it was about your shoot yesterday. He seems to be under the impression that you are a model." She made a noise he was going to assume was a cough and didn't want to think about her laughing at him. "Shall I set him straight for you?"

It took his mind nearly a full ten seconds to remember what the man could want. There had been a photographer there yesterday. Michael had been told several times that he'd been late and that he wasn't dressed the way they'd requested. Then Grace had come out dressed in that sinful robe and nothing else and he'd completely

15

forgotten. He'd refused to sign off on anything they shoved at him until he'd had his lawyer read it.

"Send him in. And Betsy, hold my calls until I'm finished with him. Also, could you please find Matt and tell him I need to see him, please? As soon as possible."

He knew she'd do it so he leaned back in his chair and waited. He had a fleeting thought that the man might not have been the one from yesterday, but doubted it. He'd been both surprised and annoyed that they thought he could be...

"Thank you for seeing me, Mr. Cunningham. I was afraid you'd have no time for me and, well, I really wanted to get your permission on these shots we took yesterday. They're simply amazing. Gracie said that I should trash them...well, we won't go into what she really said. That girl has a mouth on her, doesn't she?"

Michael couldn't have agreed more. The woman had a luscious mouth and one he decided he'd like to get another taste of. Before he could agree or disagree with the man, Matt, his long time friend and personal lawyer, walked in.

"Matthew Gray, I'd like you to meet...I'm sorry, I don't believe I caught your name." The man seemed to positively glow with his smile.

"Arnold Malone. So happy to meet you. Oh my, you should join your friend here and do some of the layouts that Gracie has in her catalogs. She would sell...well, more than she does now and she does sell a great deal."

Michael sat when Matt did. He brought him up to speed on why the man was there and asked him if he'd had a chance to look over the releases from yesterday.

"There are one or two things that I'm wondering about," Matt said with a smile. "First of all, do you have any of the shots that were taken of my cli—"

"That won't be necessary. He doesn't need to see them to—"

"Oh yes," said Arnold, completely ignoring Michael in his desperate attempt to keep his buddy from viewing the girl dressed the way she'd been. But when Arnold handed him the pictures Matt burst out laughing.

"Christ, Michael, you didn't tell me she was a beauty. And she seemed to be...enjoying herself all wrapped up around you like that. You don't seem to be minding it so much either." Matt looked through several photos before he handed them to Michael with a wink and a smile. "And what, exactly, does the woman sell? I mean, there isn't really much on her that is...marketable."

"Oh no. Gracie Anne sells women's apparel. The kind that catches a man's eye, so to speak and, from all accounts, they do seem to do that with no problem. Gracie has quite a following, I'm told. I've been doing her layouts for more than five years. She uses me for promo shots and sometimes, like with Mr. C here, for remakes. When something isn't quite what she had in mind, or if the shot is simply just too off." Arnold handed them another file, this one with photos as well as descriptions, as he continued. "This is the catalogue that goes out in a few months. She is always two seasons ahead so that it can be finished and in the homes or shops before the real season starts. Even though it is only May she is doing her Christmas catalogue now. And in November we'll shoot the spring one."

Michael looked at Matt. "Miss Waite owns the building that I want. She refuses to sell or even talk to me about prices. I went there yesterday to see if I could talk some sense into her. I ended up in those pictures instead."

Matt looked at the catalogue and then up at Michael. "Are you telling me that Gracie Anne Designs owns the Washington building?"

Michael nodded and knew that he was going to regret his next words.

"Holy fuck, man, no wonder she won't sell. She doesn't just own the building, but from all accounts, she lives there too."

~~~

Grace was sitting at her desk going over colors for the new line when she heard the stairs creak. She smiled. In a few minutes her friend would be stumbling into her room and demanding coffee. She was glad that Carol had come over, she just wasn't so happy about dealing with the morning after hang over she always had. Grace

17

didn't drink and Carol thought it was her duty as her friend to drink enough for both of them.

"Sleep well? Or do I need to ask?" She smiled when she glared at her. "Okay, I'm thinking that was a no. There's coffee brewing for you in the kitchen and there's a croissant in the box on the counter. By the way, it's nearly noon. Don't you have some sort of meeting today to be at?"

"No. I canceled when you called. What, if anything, are you going to do about that yummy man that you bitched about last night? I've heard of him. Michael Cunningham is not a man to fuck with. Maybe fuck, but certainly not fuck with." Carol stretched out on the lounger in her office. "Of course, if you did fuck him, maybe you'd feel a hell of a lot better."

"I'm just fine, thank you very much. And I'm not going to let him fuck me in either sense of the word. Now," Grace said as she tossed a pencil at Carol, "go eat and drink and leave me to this. I have to figure out which one of these fucked up pictures to use, come up with a skimpy bathing suit for this princess to wear on her honeymoon, and also figure out what sort of designs I can come up with for the spring catalogue that comes on in fourteen months."

Gracie had moved to New York right after graduation. She'd been trying to go to California, about as far away as she could from her parents, but she'd gotten on the wrong bus. And without the funds to get her back she'd ended up on the streets.

She'd worked her way from the kid who swept up after the cuttings, saving all the scraps she could, to what she was now. In those early days she'd made her designs in miniatures, sewing together the small pieces of trash to make what she liked. Years later, and yards of fabric too, she was not only making more money than she'd ever dreamed possible, but she owned the building she lived and worked in and she had people working for her.

"Grace, I can't find my shoes. Do you know where they are?"

She turned to look at her as she set a plate of pancakes on the table.

"I thought I took them off in the living room. Now they seem to have taken off on their own. And do you have anything for a flipping headache?"

She reached into her desk drawer and threw her the bottle of aspirin. She'd worked late every night to get the catalogue finished so that today was supposed to be her day. She was going to get herself a big bed and all the trimmings, curtains, comforter, and also those silk sheets she'd been eyeing for over a year now. They were flaming red and she wanted them badly.

She was in her room dressing when she thought of the catalogue. It wasn't finished. It was Saturday and she thought she'd be done with all this by now. There was still a shoot yet to take. And she had no idea why she didn't just let the guy from the guild pose for the shot and be done with it. But she couldn't. He wasn't right; no one had been right since that arrogant ass had come into her studio and fucked it up. She was just coming down the stairs from the upper levels of the five-story building when she heard Carol talking to someone. She detoured to the living room to see who it was and nearly snapped her tongue off when none other than Arrogant Ass was standing there.

"Here's Gracie now." Carol turned when she growled. "She doesn't normally sound like a dog, but she's been working a lot. Gracie, this is Mr. Cunningham. The one we were talking about last night." Carol wiggled her brows. Grace was not amused. "Well, I can see my work here is complete. I'll call you later, Gracie. Nice to meet you, Mr. Cunningham."

Carol made several gestures behind the man. All of them having to do with sex. Grace wasn't a prude, but some of them, she thought, bordered on pornographic. She tried to ignore her and focus on the man in front of her. "How did you get up here? There's a code on the door and I didn't allow you in." She glanced at the door to see if it had been broken into. "I want you to get out before I call the police."

"The guy downstairs told me that you were up here and that, since it was Saturday and I knew that you lived here, he thought you wouldn't mind me coming up. And I didn't tell him anything different." He looked around the room as he stepped further in. "Nice place."

Her mind raced to try and remember if anyone had said she lived here. She couldn't remember anyone letting it slip and was sure he'd lie his way in. She wanted to toss him out on his ear, but in all honesty she was a little afraid to get too close to him. It wasn't that she was afraid he'd hurt her, she was afraid of what she might do to him.

She'd tried hard to forget the way he'd felt against her. And more, to forget how long it had been since anyone had held her, really held her. She didn't get a lot of time to date and she figured that if one man could make her feel things that…well, she decided to go out with the first man who asked her just to get back into practice.

"I want you to leave, Mr. Cunningham. I have plans today and dealing with you is not on the list. And don't come back. I've told you numerous times I'm not going to—"

"I just want to have a conversation with you. We were…interrupted the other day and I still want you to consider the offer I'm giving you. You're keeping me from the project I have to finish and I'm trying to be nice."

She laughed. Before she could say anything a boy walked into her apartment. "Dad, I have to go to the bathroom. And you said you'd be right back." He looked from his father to her, then back again. "Please? I have to go really bad."

"Trace, this is Miss Waite. This is her place; you'll have to clear it with her." Michael looked at her with a smirk. "If she doesn't let you use her bathroom, maybe you could go…I don't know, pee in the alley."

She wanted not only to smack his face, but to knock that knowing grin off of it. She counted to ten and then smiled at the boy. "Come along, Trace. I'll take you. Maybe while we're gone your father will go down to his car and wait for you. I'm sure he's wasting his time here. In fact, I'm positive that he is." She led him down the hall and thought about how much he looked like his father.

Michael really was a beautiful man. Dark hair that was just a bit too long to be conservative and then there was the slight curl at the ends. His son, Trace, had the same dark tone, but his was curlier and longer than his dad's. They were both tall, though Michael was considerably taller at more than six and a half feet. And he was muscled. When he'd pulled her against his body she'd felt every one of them. Christ, she thought as she led the boy back to the door, she really did need to get laid.

She found him sitting on her couch. Drinking her coffee. When she and Trace came down the hall again and walked in he stood, but didn't apologize for making himself at home. She didn't know whether to smack him upside the head or…she wanted to smack his head, she decided. She walked to the door and picked up her keys.

"I'm leaving, Mr. Cunningham. And I'd very much like it if you left now so that I can lock up. As I've said, I have plenty of things to do today and you're not—"

"I'm getting a bed today," Trace said quickly. "My old one broke and I've been saving my money to get a big one. I've been saving my allowance for over a year. Why don't you come with us? You and Dad can talk and I can get my bed."

She looked at Trace. A bed? It seemed much too close to her own shopping today for her to think he hadn't been told. She thought about Carol. "Did you ask Carol what I was doing today?" She didn't believe him when he shook his head. It was the smile, she decided. "She didn't tell you I was bed shopping too?"

"No. Are you?" She nodded before she could stop herself. "Good, then we'll all go together. It's Trace's birthday. He's nine today and you wouldn't want to disappoint him on his big day, would you?"

"I thank you, but…I'm sure your son has a day planned just for the two of you." And if not, she certainly wasn't joining him. "I have a lot of errands to run as well. Then I have to go to the grocery store and—"

"My cake is at the store too," Trace told her excitedly. "We're gonna pick it up and take it to my grandma's after we're done. Will you come to my party? You can be my special date. Grandma said every man needs a special date."

"I don't...Mr. Cunningham, please tell your son that this isn't a good idea. You and I...well, we have a history that we...I don't think this is a good idea." She wanted to tap her foot while he seemed to think over his answer. When he finally did answer she was sure this was going to be the worst day of her life.

"I think it's a wonderful idea. We can talk about the building and I can help you both test out beds. I think you should have yours tested well, don't you?"

Yes, she decided, she was going to smack him. She looked down at Trace who had the most puppy dog look on his face. She knew she was lost. She looked back up at Michael and frowned. "No business. None. And the first time you mention it, I'm gone. It's my first free Saturday for over six months and I don't want to talk business. Not that you could talk me into selling anyway, but no business. Is that clear?"

"Crystal. And for the record." He was suddenly in front of her. "I don't like being told what to do—in the bedroom or out." This last part he whispered near her ear. It was everything she could do not to moan. And when he stepped back she nearly reached for him to steady herself. She was going to get laid if it was the last thing she did and it was not going to be this bastard.

Chapter 3

Michael was enjoying himself. He hadn't expected to. In fact, he'd about decided that when they'd both came down from the hallway he was going to tell them something had come up. But her telling him what he was going to do made him feel a little vindictive toward her. And when he'd crowded her in the hallway he realized that he might have bitten off more than he could chew.

And Trace was having a great time. He had a way about him that Michael could see in himself. The kid was a charmer all right, and Michael loved it. The few times he'd turned to her for advice, she'd talked to him as though he was on her level and not some stupid kid who she didn't have time for. The two of them were having a lot of fun. With each other anyway.

Grace ignored him. Well, as much as he'd let her. He had no idea why he baited her, but he enjoyed watching her bite her cheek. He knew she was doing it because Trace had told her that she was going to wear a callous there and then she'd looked like the elephant man like he'd seen on television. Michael had burst out laughing, which had earned him a glare and he was sure a few hundred dirty names in her mind. And yet, nearly three hours later, she was still with them.

"I'm going to get the blue bed with the race car. It's not too much and I'll have enough left over to get the curtains I want too."

Trace looked longingly at the bunk beds before he continued. "And I'm going to get the matching blankets, and the lamp for my desk."

She glanced at the bunk beds too. Michael was about to tell his son that he'd pay the difference when she stepped in. He was suddenly very glad he'd brought her along.

"That's a good choice. Of course, you managed to save over a thousand dollars in such a short time, right?" Trace nodded and glanced at the bunk beds again. "Maybe you could, I don't know, borrow the money from someone. I'm betting you'll get a few bucks at your party today, and you're not really that short, are you?"

Michael could see the joy leap in Trace's eyes, but he didn't jump at the idea. He'd heard them talking about how much money he'd had to spend and the difference between the bed he was getting and the one he wanted was huge. Over a grand difference.

But Michael liked the bunk beds better too. They were wooden, solid oak that had a dresser under one end and a desk the other. The second bed, the lower one, jutted out from under the first in an L shape. It was well made, practical, and the perfect thing for a kid's room. Hell, he wanted Trace to have them as well and was just on the verge of making the offer when Trace turned to him.

In ten minutes of wheeling and dealing, they had a deal. He'd work for the difference by keeping his grades up and his room clean. And, in exchange, Michael would foot the difference. In less time than it took them to pay for Trace's new bedroom set, Grace had finished up her own purchases.

Trace got the bedding for each bed and he'd even gotten himself a couple of really "coolness" rugs to set by his bed. Michael was impressed. He wasn't sure that at this boy's age, he might have been a lot more impulsive with his purchases. He even offered to pay him interest on the loan he was fronting him. He, of course, told him if he made his payments on time, then he'd be fine. For now. They were coming out of the store when Grace turned to him finally.

"Mr. Cunningham, it's been very lovely spending time with your son, but I have to get some things done. You two have a very nice rest of the day." She even held out her hand as if he would take it and then go away. He smiled at her and she took a step back.

"You've been invited to spend the day with us. I'm pretty sure that we had more plans, don't you think, Trace?" He knew he was being a bastard, but he found that he didn't want to leave her just yet and, apparently, neither did his son.

"I want you to be my date, Grace. Please? It'll be fun. All my uncles will be there and my aunts. Besides, you were sure helpful when I needed it. I have to repay you now. Besides, you hanging with us made that weird sales lady keep away. She was all over Dad the last time we were here."

Michael could feel the flush on his face at the boy's comment. The sales person had been right there with them the entire time. She'd even offered to give him her phone number—several times. Then this time there had been an occasional question answered and Grace had made sure that the answers had been directed at Trace. Something else he'd enjoyed, her putting Trace above their differences.

"Trace, I don't think your grandmother meant for you to bring a complete stranger to her house. You and your father go and have a grand time. I'll just go on from here and—" She put out her hand again just as his phone rang. It was his mom. Michael handed the cell to his son and watched Grace shift on her feet and glare at him.

"That was my grandma," Trace said as he handed the phone back to Michael. "She said you come on with us and that there will be plenty of food. And she said for you to tell Dad to behave himself. I don't know why she said that, but she said he'd understand."

Michael threw back his head and laughed. "Yes, I understand. Shall we, Grace?" He waved her toward his car.

"May I speak to you? Privately, please?" She didn't even open her mouth, her teeth clenched so tight he was sure she was going to do permanent damage to them. She told his son to wait right there, please, and not to move. He walked her to the limo and watched her bend over and climb in. He knew that he'd have that memory burned in his mind for months, if not years to come. She started in on him the moment the door was closed.

"What the hell do you think you're doing? I want you to back off. I'm going to ask you once more to leave me alone. I don't know how many ways I can—"

He yanked her to him and silenced her with his mouth. Christ, but she was made for kissing. When she moaned and touched her hand to his shoulder he shifted them so that she was sitting nearly on his lap. Lifting her leg, he pulled her onto him and tightened her to his groin. This time the moan came from him. He had never wanted anyone like he did Grace Waite. When a knock at the window stopped him from laying her back over the seat and taking her, he smiled when she whimpered as he pulled back. Another knock, this one harder, had him sitting her on the seat next to him and reaching for the controls.

"It's raining. Can we go to the store now or are you guys not finished talking?" Trace stuck his head in the window and looked at Grace. "She looks weird. Is she all right?"

"Yes. She was just showing me how much she wanted to come with me. Climb on in, buddy, before you get soaked."

Michael could tell by the look on her face that she'd gotten the double-entendre. And he was reasonably sure that he was going to pay for it too. He leaned back into the seat and told his driver to take them to the store on Tenth. They were gliding into traffic when her phone rang.

~~~

She didn't want to answer the call. She wanted to berate the man sitting next to her and then go home. He'd made her feel things that…well, she was sure she'd never felt things like that before. She decided not to think about those things when she answered.

"You fucking cunt. Do you think I can't get to you all the way up there in New York City? I can. I will. And the rest of your family will be dead too."

She didn't remember her phone being taken away from her. She could hear shouting, but none of it registered. She only knew that someone had found her. Grace tried to pull away from the man who

26

held her and the little boy she'd scared, but Michael kept dragging her back.

"Grace? Grace, tell me...Trace, give me a bottle of water for her."

She looked up at Michael.

"What is it?" he asked her.

"Nothing. It was...people like to make comments on the type of clothing I sell all the time and sometimes they...this is Trace's day. I'm not going to worry about a small-minded person when he has so much to celebrate."

She hoped that he'd understand she wasn't going to talk about it in front of his son and though he didn't ask again, she knew that he was far from satisfied. She leaned her head back against the seat and thought about what she had to do now. Now that someone had found her, found her after all she'd done to ensure they wouldn't, she would have to bolt again.

She could sell him the building. He wanted it and she needed it gone. The caller had been able to find her in New York, which wasn't all that hard, but if they knew where she was it was only a matter of time before they figured out where she was living too. And they'd found her phone number easily enough. She frowned down at the cell in her hand. It, too, would have to go. She closed her eyes against the sudden pain there. And she'd have to leave everything she knew.

She had a cart in front of her suddenly and she was checking things off her list. She had no idea what the conversations were she participated in. She thought she was giving the correct answers, but she didn't really care. She was shopping, yes, shopping for food she knew she'd never eat.

The drive to his parents' was surreal for her. She'd lived in New York for nearly ten years and had never been this far out. The houses got bigger and the lawns much more lush the more they drove. By the time they pulled around the circular drive she nearly had her face smashed up against the window.

Trace was practically bouncing off the seat when he saw the dogs come running toward them. As soon as the car stopped he was

27

out the door and tumbling in the yard with them. Before she could get a few steps away from the car Michael pulled her back toward him. She looked up at him.

"Thank you for allowing me to help with this special time for Trace. I appreciate it. But I really have no…I shouldn't be here. This is your son's birthday and you and I don't even care all that much for each other. I should just go home."

He looked at her for several seconds and didn't say anything. She turned toward the house to call someone to come and get her when he called her name. She turned back to him and waited for him to speak. He was standing next to her when he finally spoke near her ear.

"This isn't going to end however you have going through your mind. I don't know what happened, but it can't be as bad as you think it might be."

"No," she told him with a sad shake of her head. "No, Mr. Cunningham, it's much worse."

Chapter 4

Josephine Cunningham, or Joey to her friends, watched the two of them together. Actually, they weren't so much together as the girl fought to be away from Michael. But she never said anything, even with the daggers she kept throwing at him. Trace seemed to be having the time of his life with her as well.

She laughed twice when Grace elbowed her son. Michael didn't get upset, but seemed to find her avoidance of him funny. Strange, she thought. Normally, Michael backed off when someone gave him the cold shoulder. Not that it happened much, but it didn't seem to faze him now.

Joey wondered why the girl was here. Not that she minded, but it had been more than curious. Trace had asked, begged really, if he could bring her to his party. Grace had even produced a gift for him. A very nice set of lamps that Trace said would be "awesomesauce" for his room. Whatever that meant.

"Would you like some more cake, dear? There is plenty and if you don't have another piece, I won't be able to either." Joey handed her a plate of cake and sat down beside her.

"Thank you, Mrs. Cunningham. It's delicious. And thank you for allowing me to come here today." Grace took a big bite of the cake.

Joey watched her eat. She was happy to see that she didn't pick at her food, but ate with gusto. She looked over at her son before

29

she decided to dig a little information from her. The last that Joey had heard, this woman had made Michael very mad, and now here she was at his son's birthday celebration.

"Call me Joey. And thank you. My daughter-in-law made it. To be honest, I think she buys it, but she won't say." Joey took several bites before she continued. "I hope the two of them didn't force you into coming today. It was lovely that you're… I'm going to be honest and snoop. What is the relationship between you and Michael?"

Grace laughed. It was a beautiful sound and Joey noticed that Michael turned to the sound as if drawn to her and it. She smiled. Curiouser and curiouser.

"Ask your son, Mrs. Cunningham or, better yet, your grandson. I'm just here because I'd been backed into a corner. After this party I'm sure that you'll never see me again." Grace looked over at Trace and the other children. "Do you ever wonder what they think about when they play together? What could be going through their minds when they get up in the morning?"

Joey looked at the children and then back at Grace. "Mostly I just enjoy them. Their laughter and their antics. Trace is such a joy and I see him more than any of the other grandkids. He and Michael lived here with us until about six months ago. Michael now has a house closer to town and Trace comes to the offices when he gets out of school. It works out well for the both of them."

Joey waited for her to ask about Trace's mom. When she didn't, Joey wondered about it. But then she didn't have a clue what the relationship was between them, and it didn't look as though she was going to get any information from her. She watched Michael as he talked to his brothers. He seemed to keep his attention on Grace as well. Joey thought about Trace's mother.

Victoria Hamilton had been a force to be reckoned with. Joey had never thought that Michael and she suited. They fought constantly and, when they were not fighting, they were arguing. Michael had told her there was a difference in the two, though Joey had never been able to figure out what it was. There was still loud voices and name-calling. But when Victoria had told Michael she was pregnant and was getting an abortion he'd made arrangements to keep the child.

He'd paid her a great deal of money to not terminate the pregnancy and if she delivered, then he would pay her a million dollars. She'd agreed and had even signed over all rights of the baby to Michael. Eighteen months after Trace was born she had been killed in a boating accident that took the lives of two others. It had been nothing more than an accident.

"I really should be going," Grace said as she stood up a little while later. "I've called a cab. I have a lot to do tomorrow."

Joey was about to protest her leaving when Marshall, the butler, came to say there was a taxi at the gate for Miss Waite. Smiling, Joey thought she'd just let her go and not tell her son. Walking Grace to the door, she told her that she was happy to meet her and wished she'd come back soon. With a firm handshake and no reply, the girl left. She was just shutting the door behind her when Michael came into the hall.

"Where's Grace? I looked around and couldn't find her." He continued to look around as he continued. "I thought maybe I'd ask her to spend the night so that Trace could spend more time here tomorrow."

"She left," Joey said as she walked away. "She said she had a lot to do tomorrow and she—"

"What do you mean she left? How? And why did you let her get away?" He grabbed his coat and yelled at Trace he was going out. "I swear, that girl needs to listen to—"

"Michael Allen Cunningham, you wait right there." He stopped moving toward the door when she snapped. "What do you mean, 'let her get away?' I didn't realize that you'd kidnapped her and that I was somehow your accomplice."

"She is the girl that…she won't sell me the building and I thought that—"

"That you could what?" She saw him flush and realized he'd hoped to persuade her using other ways to sell it to him and to sleep with him. "You didn't."

31

"Didn't what?" He looked to the door, whether to escape or to go after Grace she wasn't sure. "I need that building and I mean to have it. And if I can go out with a beautiful woman while I'm doing it, then what's the harm?"

For whatever reason, Joey thought maybe it was more than just a building for both of them and she secretly hoped that Grace held out for as long as she could. Without a word to her son she went back into the living room. Five minutes later he came in as well. She thought maybe she'd have to go and see this building and its owner soon. Very soon, if her son was perusing her this hard.

~~~

The offer on the building was going to make disappearing so much easier. She had money, of course, but getting to it and everything else would be something she'd have to take time to do and she didn't think she had a great deal of it. She looked at the figures for what she had in cash. She'd been planning for this for a very long time and now that it was time to move she found herself reluctant to do so.

There was enough money hidden around the building for her to never have to work again. She looked at the glossy pictures hanging on the walls. There were the covers to her catalogues along with every magazine cover she'd ever been on or even in. And there were a great many of them. She would simply have to leave everything behind. Including the new bed, which there was no way to cancel the order for.

She wanted to call her sister. She wanted to call Jazzie and tell her…everything. But she couldn't. She hadn't been able to tell them when she'd been down on her luck and homeless, nor had she been able to tell them when she'd made it big. They'd known, of course. There was no way not to when they knew who she was, but this person who'd called… Grace knew things too. Things that were scary. Things that she still had trouble believing. She knew more about her mom than a child should ever know.

Grace shuddered when she thought of the woman who'd given birth to them all. The woman who, on occasion, would do things that not only seemed out of character for the whipped woman, but bordered on insanity. She knew exactly what her mother was and she also knew most of the players involved.

Her mother had split personality disorder, or sometimes known as disambiguation. She knew that there was at least three other "people" that her mother lived with. Ginny was one and the most prominent. Then there was Verrie, one who only showed herself when things were too tense for the other two to cope, and Guinnie. Verrie was by and far the most violent and she would just as soon kill you as to look at you.

Guinnie was the one that seemed the most childlike. She rarely came out, Grace was sure, and the only times that Grace had seen her was when one of Guinevere's children were hurt or ill. She was the one who'd told Grace about the others.

Guinevere Waite was insane. Not only that, but Grace was afraid she was also a killer. Grace had seen things, heard things, that made her run. Even after the rape when she was seventeen she'd not been as afraid as she'd been when she heard the screams coming from her parents' room. Screams that still, to this day, made the hair on her arms rise and the back of her neck feel like something was dancing there.

It had been the night before her graduation. She'd been in her room daydreaming about the day she'd be able to leave home for good. Her sister Jazzie was asleep and the other two, Sin and Lilliane, were watching television in the bathroom so they wouldn't get caught. At first she thought it was coming from the bathroom, but when she got up to tell them to turn it down the noise got quieter. She went into the hallway and listened.

The moaning made her think her parents were having sex and she nearly turned back to her room and then the bath to throw up, but then she remembered her father was in jail again. Grace, knowing that she would regret it, tiptoed down the hall to the shut bedroom door.

The moaning was so low she had to press her ear to the door to hear it. Now, even after all these years, she wondered why she didn't just think her mom was having an affair and leave it at that.

But she didn't. Couldn't, if the truth be told. She was still listening at the door when she heard the *pop.*

Standing stock still Grace knew that it was a gun shot. And when the second, then the third pop sounded, she heard her mother laughing hysterically. It took her several seconds, too many for her to get back to her room, before she realized that someone was turning the knob on the door. She'd just had time to press back against the wall when the door opened.

There she stood. Her mother was naked and covered in...Grace had always hoped she'd imagined the blood that dripped from her mother's elbows as she walked down the hall toward the closet. But as she turned her head and looked in between the door and the jamb that opened into her parents' room, she saw the man lying there.

He was naked as well as covered in blood. But his was pooling beneath him. The dark stained the rug that he lay on and the sheet that lay next to him. There was an axe in his chest and a gun lying beside him. But what had Grace putting her hand over her mouth and silently sobbing behind it was that he was looking at her. There was no doubt that his dead eyes were staring right directly at her.

When her mother came back down the hall, a stack of towels in her arms, Grace heard her muttering about the man. Also about the mess he'd made and that when "Ginny" came back she'd have a fit.

"Better get a start on it or there will be hell to pay," she said in a voice that Grace remembered from the rape. "Yeppers, gotta make sure things are in order or she'll not let me come out and play again."

When the door shut, again, behind her mother, Grace stood there for several minutes. It was too much. All of it was too much. When she felt safe enough to move she went to the room she shared with her sisters and changed her clothes. Gathering up all the money she could find, even some that didn't belong to her, she left without a word to anyone.

She didn't call the police, though she probably should have. But she was terrified. And sickened. Then, when she'd been in New York for a while, she'd tried to convince herself that she'd been

34

dreaming. But that had never felt right. She knew with all her heart that her mother, or one of her others, had killed that man.

Grace got up and pulled the plank of wood from the floor. She took out the small metal box, sat back, and opened it. Inside was a list of every place she'd hid money throughout the building, a gun that she kept loaded and had never used, and several new identities. She frowned when she thought she should have used them at the beginning of her career and not the end. She looked over the new names and decided she wouldn't choose one until she was ready to leave, and put them back in the box. She opened the small notepad and looked over the list. It wasn't until she stood up that she realized how late it was. Two in the morning was no time to start this big of a project. She tucked it all back in the box and put it under her bed. After replacing the wood she stripped down and climbed into bed. The first nightmare hit her an hour later.

Chapter 5

Matt was sitting in his office going over the monthly reports when his phone rang. He simply reached over and pushed the intercom button without taking his eyes from the sheet of figures. His secretary, who was also his wife, Stacey, was speaking to someone when he tuned into her voice.

"...for so long. You've no idea. And last month's catalogue was simply a work of art. I would love to see one of those put together. You have an eye for color, Miss Waite."

"Thanks, and it's Grace." There was a pause. "I think he answered you."

"Oh my," his wife said. "Hello, honey. I have someone here who would like to speak to you. It's Grace Waite. She said that it's about the Washington building." And then she laughed. "She said to tell you if you called Michael all bets were off."

Matt was just on the verge of telling her to call Michael when she'd said that. So, the two of them hadn't worked out their differences, huh? Matt stood up and walked toward his door after telling his wife to send Miss Waite in. He winked at his wife when she walked in with Grace and hoped she'd get the message to call him anyway. With a small nod she told Grace again that she was happy to have met her.

"She's going to call him, isn't she?" Grace said as she sat in the chair at his small conference table. "I have no idea why I even

37

bothered. He does pay your check and you have to follow his rules no matter how much I hate it."

Matt laughed. "Yes. She's probably telling him to come in on one pretense or another. He'll be acting surprised, but not too over the top."

He thought he heard her say "arrogant ass," but wasn't sure if it had been directed at him or Michael and decided he didn't care. He asked her if she wanted anything and after she'd told him she was fine, he sat across from her.

"Should we wait on him or just dive right in? I'm not in any mood to have to repeat myself and, if he comes in, I'm going to be pissy with him enough as it is." She pulled out a file from her large, brightly-colored purse and pushed it across to him. "You might as well get a head start. I want that much for the Washington building and not one cent less."

Matt tried to hide his surprise, but he was sure she could see the shock. They'd been trying since Monday to contact the woman, but she'd been avoiding them. And now here it was Thursday and she was right here with a contract. Matt opened it and was on the second page of the impressive thing when Michael walked in.

"Hey, I was wondering if you wanted to grab some—oh, I didn't realize you had company. Hello, Grace. I've—"

"She knew you were coming. Figured it out before she sat down," Matt cut his friend off. "She wants to sell. I'm just going over the contract now."

Michael sat at the table near Grace. Matt laughed a little, distracted by the contract, but still found humor in that the girl didn't seem to care for his buddy. Stacey walked in with a carafe of coffee, bottled water, and a tray of Danish. She was out again before he could thank her.

"Why?" Michael said as he poured coffee for them all. "After all this time you're suddenly going to sell me what I've been wanting for six months? I don't get it. You've gotten a better offer or you're going to demand more money, is that it? Or does this have anything to do with the phone call?"

The girl paled and, before Matt could tell his friend to back off, Grace snapped right back. He was suddenly glad that he was going to get a front row seat to Michael getting his ass handed back to him on a platter.

"You egotistical, overbearing, pigheaded prick. You practically hound me to death over this fucking building and, when I come here with a legitimate offer, you act all superior and as if it's beneath you." She stood up when he did, but she didn't wait for him to move from the chair before she was shoving him back down into it. "I knew this was going to be a mistake trying to deal with a man whose ego is bigger than his bank account. You wanted the fucking building so either buy it or fucking don't. I could care less."

When she stepped away from the table and Michael, Matt started to rise and stand between the two of them before Michael followed through on what looked like murder gleaming in his eye. But he knew the moment that he'd touched Grace, a simple hand on her elbow to steer her away and to safer ground, that he'd made a mistake. Her fist came around so quickly that he'd had only a moment to be impressed with the fact that she'd tucked her thumb in before his face exploded.

He wasn't sure how he'd ended up on the floor with Michael cussing under him. He wasn't even sure what the hell Michael was doing in his office. He knew he'd hit his head; there was no way he was going to even consider that Grace had knocked him out, but things were beginning to come back to him about the time that Stacey came in the office looking decidedly unhappy with them both. That was when Matt realized that Grace was gone.

"What the hell is wrong with you?" Michael said as he helped Matt to stand up. "What the hell did you think you were doing standing between the two of us? I had it under control."

Matt wanted to point out that he most certainly did not have anything under control, but his wife was saying he was bleeding. The shrill whistle from the doorway had them all stop everything. He groaned; the sound of Mrs. Cunningham's two finger trill had his head feel every decibel of it.

39

"Would someone like to tell me why I nearly got run down by Miss Waite on her way out of this office, my attorney is bleeding to death on the nice, new carpet, and my son...well, *you,* I can figure out. You've pissed her off again, haven't you?"

Matt felt the ice pack hit his sore head and was both grateful and relieved when it felt better.

"I most certainly did not piss her off. She was already mad when she came in here." Michael turned to Matt. "He can tell you. She started on me the moment I walked in the door."

Matt decided that he'd had enough for the day and stood up. "I'm not answering that on the grounds that I would have to fight you again because I won't agree with you. You snapped, end of story. Mrs. Cunningham," he said to her with a smile. "Perhaps you could speak with the lovely Miss Waite and see what she is willing to negotiate on the price and other things she's listed on the contract she took with her."

"I'll deal with her," Michael said, but Matt cut him off.

"If you want that building, then I suggest you stay the hell away from her. You and she seem to rub each other the wrong way, contrary to the way you two heated up the pages of those pictures." Matt grabbed up is briefcase and his jacket as he headed to the door with the ice pack still on the back of his head. "And if you want my advice, sign the release forms and let her use the pictures. They could go a long way into making her believe you might actually have a brain in that fucking head of yours."

Matt was nearly to the elevator when he felt his wife next to him. She was grinning and he grinned back. She didn't say anything until the doors shut behind them and they were moving to the floors below.

"Wow, she certainly is a match to our Michael, isn't she?" She grinned again. "And she is going to give me a discount on some of the line she has at her building. Miss Waite is going to be my new best friend."

"Mine, too, if she and Michael can work this out." He winced when he moved the pack again. "She has a hell of a left, I'll give her that. Not that she took me out, I did trip over Michael, but damn."

40

Stacey's laughter made him smile again. "Sure she didn't. I would guess a little bitty girly girl like her wouldn't be able to take out a big, bad man like you."

Matt wasn't sure, but he thought she was making fun of him. He didn't really care. Not if she looked at him like she was. He slid into her car, closed his eyes, and thought about the woman who punched nothing at all like a little bitty girly-girl, but a longshoreman on a three-day leave looking for a brawl.

~~~

Grace hated to lose her temper. And when she did it made her cry, and that just wouldn't do. She wiped again at the tears and looked out the window of the cab she'd flagged down outside the building. She shouldn't have lost her temper.

The phone calls were getting worse. And the horrible part was that whoever it was had her home phone and her business line as well. She hadn't even answered any phone for several days. Monday had been bad enough. She'd been right, someone had found her.

Long ago she'd had a phone number that she'd given everyone, including her mother. The phone calls from California had been frequent back then; her mother would call for money and Grace, stupidly, would send her some. Her father would call to tell her that she needed to be more dutiful and she would simply hang up on him. Until later, that was.

About five years ago she'd stopped giving her parents anything, including speaking to them. Guinevere had become verbally abusive. And not just that, but her father had threatened her physically as well. Grace had never let her family come to visit her and, in the beginning, had had a nice apartment, but she'd since moved into the warehouse and had a security system put in. Her father had been to see her more than once and had called her to tell her to let them come stay with her, to recoup their losses. Grace had refused.

Then he'd been killed. Not his fault, her mother had said. He'd been a victim of the whore, Alyssa. If she'd done this or that, he'd be alive. And then Ginny and Verrie had started calling her too.

That was when she'd had her phone disconnected and her number made private. She'd told her sisters and brother not to give Guinevere her number and she'd been fairly happy since. Until the day of Trace's birthday party.

Grace glanced at the phone on her way past it. She didn't bother listening to the twenty-five messages. They were probably the same as they'd been all week. She was going to die. Her days were numbered, and the one that scared her the most was the one telling her what she'd had on that day and then the way the person was going to peel her skin off her. Grace went to the refrigerator, pulled out the pitcher of tea, and poured a glass. The buzzer at her door had her scream. Shaking, Grace went to the video-cam to see who was there.

Mrs. Cunningham stood there with a large man and Trace. Grace leaned her forehead against the wall and thought about just simply not answering, but when she heard her phone ring behind her she suddenly wanted company, even if it was the Cunninghams.

Without bothering to say anything Grace released the lock and watched as the three of them walked in. She'd met Mr. Cunningham at the party, so she knew who he was. She went to the kitchen again and looked for something to give to Trace, who she knew would be hungry. Kids that her employees had were always hungry at that age. She let them in when she'd unearthed a bag of her favorite cookies.

"I have no idea what it is you think you might want from me, but if you want to agree to the sale of the building then I'll sign it for you and you can be on your merry way." Grace sat on the couch and Trace gobbled up the cookies as he sat next to her.

"No, I don't want to discuss the building. Though now that I'm here, I can see why you were reluctant to sell. It's beautiful, isn't it?" Joey sat on the other couch and looked around. "I love all the color. You must get that from what you do."

Grace had a headache and she'd not been sleeping well or, she thought, maybe she might have been a little more polite. Instead, she simply asked what she wanted. The woman laughed and Trace grinned at her.

"Grandma wants to see where you make your stuff." Trace winked at her from the same beautiful eyes that his father had. "So when she and Granddad picked me up from school, we came right over."

Grace didn't want to show them around. Not today. They'd had a terrible morning which had progressed into a worse afternoon. And her temper hadn't helped. When she'd snapped at Becky for the fourth time about something stupid her assistant had called it a day and sent everyone home. Probably a good thing or Grace might have fired them all. She had to do that soon enough anyway, but not just yet.

"It's a mess down there. I've been…I have a catalogue to finish and it's not going well." Grace stood when Joey did. "I guess you can look around."

They'd been in the lower two floors for about ten minutes when she felt someone staring at her. She looked up to see Michael coming toward her with Trace. She knew that boy had let him in and couldn't be upset with him. He was his father, after all. She started to herd her guests toward the doors and out when he came up beside her.

"May I speak to you, please, alone?"

She shook her head at his request.

"Please? I'll be polite and I promise not to piss you off. Well, I'll try not to piss you off."

She turned away from his attempt at humor. "I'm having a bad day, Mr. Cunningham. And I have a headache from hell. Whatever you want is in the contract. If you have any questions I'm sure my attorney would be more than happy to listen to you."

"Grace, please. I want to speak to you about your family." She looked at him sharply then at the phone that started ringing. Before she could get to it he moved to the desk. The voice at the other end sent chills down her spine.

"Did you really think I'd not find you? You're as stupid as those cunt sisters of yours if you thought that. When I find you, and never doubt that I will, I'm going to enjoy killing you. Killing you so that I can get what I want."

Michael picked up the phone as the person continued. "Who is this?" He looked at her and paled. Then he put the phone down in the cradle and walked toward her. Stalked would have been a better term. "Come with me. Now."

She suddenly found herself in her office. It was cramped and with him in the room, it seemed smaller. When she was sitting on her little couch with her head between her knees she saw her tears falling to her shoes. She didn't want to cry in front of this man more than any other person she'd known.

"I get those sorts of calls all the time," she told him from her bent position. "It's not that big of deal. And you had no right to answer—"

"She knew my son's name. She told me that if I was smart, I'd take Trace away from here before whoever it was came after him too."

She brought her head up and looked at him as he continued.

"Now, we're going to calmly talk about this and you're going to tell me truthfully if this is the reason you're selling this building to me."

The knock at her office door didn't really give her any reprieve. She'd hoped that his family wanted to go and they wanted him to come with them, but she wasn't that lucky. Michael told them that they'd meet them in the restaurant and that she and he would be there soon. The door was closed again before she could voice that she wasn't going anywhere.

Chapter 6

Michael watched her as she stared at her lap. He wanted to pick her up and shake the truth from her, but knew that he'd only upset her more. Instead, he looked around the small office. He was both impressed and horrified at what was there.

The desk was huge. He couldn't believe how big. But he could see that it was more of a workstation with a computer than it was a working desk. He didn't know why, but he thought she'd have her real desk, one that she'd do her business on, somewhere on the upper floors. This one was for putting together her business.

The array of colors around the room were a little too much for him, but the more he stared at them, the more he could see that they weren't just thrown about like he'd first thought, but in an order that he could see now had been thought out, colors and patterns together along with buttons, zippers, and other things like ribbons and things; he'd never guess what they were in a million years. The mannequins, several of them with materials draped over them in layers, stood in a long line; a large container of scissors sat on a tray along with a stapler and rolls of tape. She was designing things with not only style, but with colors, patterns, and accessories. He turned back to her when she started to speak.

"If you just leave me alone they'll leave you alone too. They only threatened you because you...they think you might mean something to me. I'm sure that once you buy the building—"

"You think you can hide from them and that selling me the building will give you the money to do it, don't you?" When she looked at him he could see the truth of his words in her face. "It won't work. They may give up on Trace and myself, but they will eventually find you again and then what? Do you want to keep running from it, or simply wait until they find some other family you attach yourself to in order to get to you?"

"I never asked you and your family to come here. I never asked you to bring your son into my life that day. I was doing just fine until you had to have my building." She stood up and he nearly smiled at the fire. He liked this much better than the beaten girl she'd just been.

"No, you didn't. But now we are." He watched her pace and tried to regain control of his wayward thoughts, thoughts of stripping her down and seeing what delights she had on under those soft, flannel pants and t-shirt. "Who is it that was on the phone and how many calls have you received?"

Her laugh was short and harsh. "You mean today or just over the past week? Never mind, it doesn't matter. Suffice it to say that there have been numerous. I'm selling, Mr. Cunningham. If you want this building, then tell me now or it goes on the market. Your choice."

Michael stood and walked to her. He wanted the building, but right now, right this moment, all he could think about was her leaving him. He didn't know why that thought was there, but he suddenly didn't want her gone. She backed away as he moved closer.

"Hasn't anyone ever told you not to run from a predator? As prey, you would do better to gather your forces and make a stand." He pulled off his jacket and tossed it toward the chair. "There are greater strengths in numbers, Grace."

"I know what I'm doing." He moved closer as he pulled his tie loose and left it hanging. He toed off his shoes as he moved. "Unless you plan to try on one of the dresses over there you'd better stop taking off clothes."

Her voice had gotten huskier and low. He felt it as though she'd touched him, ran her voice along his skin, and caressed him. He unbuckled his belt and pulled it free of the loops. "No. I'm not going to try on dresses. Take off your shirt, Grace. It's making me crazy trying to imagine what you have on beneath it." She didn't move, but he could see her nipples harden. "Grace, take off the shirt or I will."

She backed up several steps as he moved closer. She stopped when she backed against the long counter behind her. When he was about a foot from her he reached out, ran his fingers over her breast, and never took his eyes from hers.

"Are you bare beneath here? I can feel the lace of something and it makes my mouth water to taste you." He lifted her breast in his hand and watched her eyes flutter closed. "Watch me, Grace. Watch while I suckle at your nipple and taste you."

Michael stepped the last foot to her, lifted her by her ass, and sat her on the counter. Her legs opened and he moved between them and pulled her shirt over her head all in one move. He was so wrong about the lace beneath. It was more than he could have imagined.

The strapless bit of sex was black. Silky black lace that was filled with her heavy flesh and left her nipple bare. He moaned at how tight her dark nipples were and how long. He leaned down and took the hard tip into his mouth as her fingers laced in his hair. Christ, he was in heaven.

She was warm and tasted like fresh strawberries. Spreading his hand at her back, he pulled her closer as he moved his mouth up to her throat and to her shoulder. Nipping at her, he felt her legs wrap around him and he rocked them both against the ledge. Taking her mouth, devouring her, he turned them to find something, anything he could take her against. He looked at the desk and realized that even for the small size of the room, the desk was simply too far away. He lowered them to the floor.

Her hands parted his shirt; buttons flew everywhere as she tore her mouth from his and took his nipple into her mouth. He moaned when she bit him, his cock aching now to feel her clamped around him as he pounded into her. He sat up on his knees to open his pants

47

while she pulled her pants down to her hips, lifted both legs up, and pulled them off. Michael grabbed her legs as she tossed away her pants and panties and wrapped her ankles at his shoulders.

"Are you protected? I don't have protection, but if I'm not inside of you soon, I'm going to explode all over you."

"Yes, no…I'm safe. I'm on the pill." She moaned as he moved his cock at her soaking entrance. "Please, fuck me."

Keeping her legs up, he bent her back and entered her. She was tight and hot; her walls clenched at him, rippled along his cock as he moved in and out. Michael wanted to come now, felt his balls tighten against his body even as he let her legs go and they wrapped once again around his hips. He leaned down and over her and took her mouth again before moving down to suckle at her luscious nipple.

Her scream of release had him throwing back his head as he followed her. He rocked as he jettisoned into her. Every part of his body came; he'd never felt such an orgasm in his life and, as he dropped his weight on top of her, he realized that he wanted her again.

Rolling to his back, Michael took her with him. His pants were still around his legs, so he shimmed out of them and held her. His cock, still buried in her, stirred when she moaned, but he was sure he needed a little more time before he could take her again. When she stretched he thought maybe he'd need less than he'd thought. When she looked down at him, her chin resting on her fist, he thought maybe he could get used to this.

"This doesn't change anything. It was really good sex, but I'm still going to leave."

He smiled at her words.

"If you want the building then tell me now."

"Grace, I don't know how other men have reacted to your bossy ways, but you'll find I'm much bossier. You and I just had incredible sex, not good sex, and I for one plan to do it a lot more." He rolled her to her back and rocked his hips into her. "Now would be nice, but my family is—Christ."

She bit his neck and tightened around him. When she wrapped her legs around him and surged up Michael's eyes crossed. Before he knew it he was being pushed to his back and she was astride him.

With her hands on his chest she rode him. Watching her face as she enjoyed herself, Michael found himself mesmerized by her. With her eyes closed he could still read every time she hit her sweet spot; her breasts flushed and her nipples hardened. When she moved her hands along his waist to her hips then moved to her pussy he nearly came watching her. As she slid her finger along her clit she surged forward and moaned. Michael watched as she lifted her free hand, cupped her breast, and rolled her nipple.

"Your cock feels wonderful," she practically moaned at him. "I'd forgotten how good a real cock can feel deep inside of me." She leaned back and her hair brushed over his thighs. Michael gripped her hips tighter to him. "Oh, Christ, I'm coming."

She grabbed his hands and held him as she rode faster. Her breasts, flushed now, bounced and bobbed; her nipples lengthened. Sitting up, he took one peak into his mouth and bit her. Her scream of his name had him rolling her over and fucking her hard, each stoke of his cock pulling deeper and deeper until he came. Michael was sure that this woman was not getting away from him, no matter what.

~~~

Grace stepped out of the shower and heard Michael speaking. She closed her eyes and wondered what he was still doing here. Especially in her bedroom, especially after what they'd done in her office downstairs. Grace wiped the moisture off the mirror and looked at herself.

He'd bruised her. There were marks on her neck from his mouth and more along her breasts and hips. She shuddered when she remembered his mouth there and how tightly he'd held her as he'd come. Grace turned her back to her reflection and started to pull on clothes. As soon as she got dressed she was showing him the door and locking him out of her house and out of her life. She didn't need this right now. The phone ringing had her pulling on one sock

49

and rushing out the door. He was just picking it up when she came out.

"Yes, this is Gracie's house. She was in the shower…I'm sure that's none of your business, but I'm reasonably sure that she's a bit over twenty-one and no longer needs a—I see. Yes, I can see where, as her brother, you'd think that, but again—"

Grace tried to take the phone from him before he told Cain…well, she didn't want him to tell her brother anything, thank you very much. But he pulled her against him and buried his face into her shoulder. She forgot what she'd been doing until he spoke again.

"Yes," he growled, and she wasn't sure who he was talking to until he continued. "Yes, she's here. If you give me a minute to kiss her again I'll let you talk to her."

The phone was suddenly on the small end table and she was being lifted against Michael's body. His mouth seemed to be everywhere. Before she could catch her breath or even try to stop him, she was pressed against the wall and Michael was nipping at her ear.

"It's your brother. He wants to speak to you." He licked along the column of her throat. "I need to get you out of this room or we'll never leave it. Talk to him and I'll be in the kitchen with ice packs on my nuts."

She giggled and he kissed her quickly. He stepped away only to return and yank her to him and kiss her again. He was stalking away from her when he barked "phone" at her. Grace picked up the phone to hear her brother talking to Alyssa.

"…thinks he is to tell me that he is going to kiss her… No, I didn't catch his name. That's a good idea, that way I can hunt him down and castrate him. Lousy bastard. Gracie," he shouted, and had her jerking the phone from her ear.

"I'm right here. Damn it, Cain, what the hell was that for? Now I'll probably have permanent hearing loss." She grinned when he growled. "If you only called to be nasty to me then I don't care to—"

"Who was that man and what is he doing answering your phone? I demand that you tell me—" Before Grace could blast her brother, she could hear Alyssa talking in the background and she didn't sound any happier. When she got on the phone next, Grace was still steaming.

"He's a bully," she told Alyssa. "And nosey. Why does he think it's any of his business what I do in my own home? He does know he's not my dad, right?"

"Yes, I'm sure he does. Or at least he'll have a better understanding once I get off here." Alyssa laughed. "He loves you and worries. He wants you here with the rest of them."

Grace felt her heart ache with the knowledge that she couldn't. Not now. She sat down and fingered the bra that Michael had torn from her last night and tossed it in the trash when her body reacted to that.

"I have a business to run. And...why did he call anyway? You're all married now so that can't be it. I already know that Lilliane is pregnant and that Sin and Payton are adopting another child. Is it Quinn now, or you who is pregnant?"

"No, though, I think maybe Jazzie is about to bust with the news that they are. He wants you to come home next weekend. All of us are getting together for dinner at our house and he wanted you there." There was a very long pause before she spoke again. "You can even bring home the man that has Cain all worked up. Does he get you all worked up too?"

Grace flushed. "Yes, he does. Though it's none of your business. He's just..." She wasn't sure what he was, but she didn't want to tell her sister-in-law that. "He's a fling."

Alyssa laughed and Grace started to say something when she looked up and saw Michael standing in the doorway. He looked like every woman's dream of a handsome prince and bad boy all in one.

"Then all the more reason to bring him here. I'm sure Cain will have a cow about it, but right now I think he'd rather have you here."

Grace didn't think getting Michael involved with her family was a good idea. He might have been able to handle them, but he

51

had a son, and Trace couldn't. She told Alyssa that she'd think about it and call her later. She hung up before she could say any more.

Chapter 7

"Your brother is worried I'm some sort of monster," Michael told her softly. "He was upset that I was in your bedroom. How did he know where I was?"

"This phone only rings in here. Cain has always been overly protective of us girls." She reached down, pulled off the one sock, and tossed the pair of them on the bed. "You need to go. I don't...I don't want you here anymore."

He didn't move, but she could see his body stiffening. His cell phone going off made her wish whoever it was would leave them alone and take him away at the same time. He didn't move to answer it.

"That might be important. Shouldn't you answer it?" She waited for an answer and, when none came, she walked to her dresser and started pulling her brush through her hair. "I'll follow you out and lock up. If you could have the contract changes to my attorney as soon as—"

"Who was the person who threatened my son?"

The question was so quiet that she almost thought she'd not heard him, but when she looked over her shoulder at him she could see that he had asked. She should have expected the question. She had been thinking about an answer to give him when he did. But nothing came to mind. Nothing, that was, but the truth and, that, she wasn't really willing to share with a man she'd only had sex with.

"I don't know, not really. I've been..." Could she tell him? Should she? "Once I leave, then you won't have anything to worry about with Trace. He'll be fine. They're just trying to get me to be afraid."

"And are you?"

She felt the tears at his question, but tried to blink them away.

"Grace, are you afraid of the person who calls you? And I've listened to the messages on your phone in the kitchen. They're getting progressively worse and you know it."

She thought about telling him it was none of his business, but she knew that the two of them having sex and whoever it was threatening Trace made it his. She didn't like it, but he had a right to know some of what she had going on.

"I left home when I was seventeen. It was...my family life wasn't all that easy. Had it not been for my brother and sisters I'm not sure how things would have ended. My parents were more into each other and how badly they could hurt us than they were at providing for us as a family. My father was killed by the police when he tried to kill my sister for ransom."

"Roscoe Waite. Matt just told me you're related to him. And Alyssa Howard is your sister-in-law." He moved up behind her, took the brush, and began moving it through her hair. "I also know your brother-in-law, Payton. We went to school together."

She nodded. Of course. Payton's family had money, as did Alyssa. She was just a daughter of a dead ex-con who happened to be related to them all. She turned and took the brush from him. "I think you should go now. I have some things to finish up around here before I sell and, if you don't mind, I want to be alone."

"I don't think so, Grace. I'll purchase the building because I need it, but you're not going anywhere. I don't know what it is about you, but I can't seem to get enough of you." He took the brush from her and set it on the dresser. "Finish getting dressed and we'll meet my family. They're waiting dinner on us."

She supposed as they were getting into his limo again that she could have refused. But short of throwing him out, which she was reasonably sure she couldn't do anyway, she wasn't sure what to do.

She wasn't even sure she wanted him to leave her alone. It had been so long since she'd...she'd had anyone in her life that she was a little starved for the feeling again. Neither of them spoke on the short drive over.

Trace meeting her at the door of the restaurant made her hug him a little tighter than was probably necessary. He held her hand, talking a mile a minute as he led them to the table overflowing with people. She stopped and felt Michael bump into her from behind.

"This is my family, you know them," he said in her ear when she didn't move. "Come on and sit down. They won't bite." But he did.

"Grace, honey, come on," his mother said as she waved at the only two empty chairs next to her. "Michael, go and find that lovely little waitress and tell her what you and Grace are drinking. Then we'll order as soon as you're served."

Michael pulled out her chair and kissed her on the mouth before he moved to do what his mother said. Grace felt her face flame when Joey laughed. She wanted to hunt the stupid man down and smack the shit out of him.

"I guess you two worked out your differences." Grace flushed again at Joey's statement. "I'm glad. You two fighting was getting to be annoying."

"I don't know what you're talking about, Mrs. Cunningham. Your son and I are simply coming to terms on the Washington Building, nothing more." Grace continued, though she was sure she was only making it worse. "He just kissed me because he knew it would irritate me. He's forever doing stupid things like that to get on my last nerve."

"He can be like that, yes. But he usually only gets on a woman's last nerve at the end of a relationship, not at the beginning," Mr. Cunningham said with a smile. "And they usually are so besotted with him they will let him break it off without much fuss. Women like our Michael."

Grace knew that Lucas Cunningham wasn't really Michael's father. He'd adopted him when Joey and Lucas had gotten married twenty-five years ago. Michael had been around five and he and

Joey had been living in a smallish apartment when the then millionaire Lucas had bought the building they'd lived in. Instead of tossing the young mother and boy out into the street he'd set them up in a nice place and began courting Joey.

When Michael returned she was gathering up her things to leave. He would just have to explain what was not going on between them on his own. She stood up just as he pulled her into his lap. She squealed as he clamped his hand around her middle.

"Sit," he growled in her ear, "or I'll tell them about the beautiful tattoo you have over your lovely ass. And I'll tell them how I happened to know that your nipples get really dark when you're aroused."

She glared at him as he laughed. She knew in that moment he'd do it too. She moved to the other chair again, vowing that she wasn't going to speak to him. Turning in her chair to face his mother she heard him laugh. She closed her eyes on the sudden urge to pick up her fork and stab him in the cock with it.

"If you do to him whatever is going on in your head, know that he'll get you back. He's never been one to let go of a challenge."

Grace looked at Joey when she smiled.

"He's got it bad for you, doesn't he?"

"I don't think it's any more than just sex. And he wants something from me. I've already told him I'll sell him the building. He's just doing this because, for some reason, he wants to prolong the inevitable. I am leaving, Mrs. Cunningham. I have to." Grace had to get away before the temptation to lean on him became more than she could bear.

"Hummm. I suppose, but I don't think you believe that any more than he does." Joey patted her hand. "As for the sex part, I'm reasonably sure you and he will come to some understanding on that as well."

~~~

Thomas watched the girl with his mother. He didn't know why, but he didn't like her. That didn't mean he wouldn't have her. Just for the simple fact that she belonged to Michael, he'd have her under him. He liked having and taking things that belonged to his stepbrother. But good Christ, this one was beautiful.

Her dark hair and darker eyes made him think of hard sex. Her body looked like something he'd only seen in magazines and he knew those girls had been touched up. But this one, Grace, looked like she'd never had any work done and he was willing to bet his brother knew it. Thomas reached under the table to adjust his cock again.

He turned to look at Michael when he said something to his dad. They were talking about money again like it was all there was to talk about. His brother had this fine-looking woman next to him and all he was doing was putting his arm around her chair and practically ignoring her. He leaned over the table to speak to Grace.

"How about you move over to this side and I'll talk to you. When Mike and my dad get to talking about spread sheets, there could be a bomb going off and they'd not hear it."

She smiled at him.

"Come on, you know you want to."

"Thanks, but this is fine." She smiled at him again and he felt some of his anger fade. "You're Thomas, aren't you? I remember you from the party."

"Yes. I'm the baby. My mother has these things where we're all required to come at least once a week. It's mostly at her house, but she's having the house done up for my sister's baby shower tomorrow." He tried not to sneer at his sister who looked like a giant frog in her green maternity dress. "This is her first one and my other sister thought it would be fun to get a bunch of her friends together and have a girl's day." Thomas didn't understand the need for a pregnant woman to show herself. He neither thought they were beautiful nor glowing. They looked bloated, fat, and clumsy. He tried his best to steer clear of all of them, especially when they got as obese as his sister seemed to be.

"That'll be nice for her. I understand her husband is fighting overseas. She must get fairly lonely without him."

Thomas looked at his sister and tried to remember if he'd been told that Jake had been transferred. He remembered someone saying something about him leaving, but he'd thought he was going to the mall or some other shit.

"Yeah, I suppose she does." Like he cared. "But she has all those servants in the house, so I doubt she gets all that lonely."

Thomas noticed that Michael moved his hand down under the table. He wondered if his brother was copping a feel from Grace. When she closed her eyes he could just imagine his own hand sliding up under her dress and feeling her wet pussy. She'd be very wet for him, he decided, and he'd make her come with everyone around.

Michael laughed at something and leaned over and whispered in Grace's ear. He didn't doubt that they were talking about him, and Thomas decided that he would find a way to take her from his stepbrother and fuck her in front of him as soon as possible.

When Grace got up a few minutes later and said she'd be back, Michael stood with her. He thought maybe the two of them were going together when, after she left the room, he sat down. But he watched her like he was going to make sure she went to the bathroom. It wasn't a minute later when he decided he was going to see if he could persuade her to have a little fun with him when Michael stood and followed Grace. Thomas wanted to scream out his frustrations and was about to go after them both when his dad put his hand on his shoulder.

"Stay here and leave them alone. You've no business sniffing around that woman when she came here with your brother."

Thomas glared at his dad.

"I don't want to have to tell you again to leave her alone."

"I wasn't going to touch her. And besides, she didn't look all that thrilled about being with Mike anyway. Maybe she'd like to have a real man with her and not some bastard you adopted."

Thomas knew he'd gone too far the moment the words left his mouth. He'd said that before to his father, not those exact words, but close enough. He and Michael had been fighting over a car then. The fact that Thomas hadn't wanted the dark blue Mustang until his dad had sold it to Michael was beside the point. He didn't think that Michael should have anything that belonged to his dad. He'd told his dad that a bastard shouldn't be allowed to sully the car that had been his father's, much less his name. His father had slapped him right across the mouth and told him to never say anything like that again. To this day Thomas had never forgiven Mike for turning his father against him.

His father turned away from him, but not before Thomas could see the disappointed look in his eyes. He just had one more reason to hate his brother. For giving him a reason to disappoint his father.

Thomas decided that he was going to get back at Michael. He wasn't sure how, but he knew it was going to have to be big. He glanced over at Trace when he felt someone staring at him, and he glared at the kid. That brat saw way too much and, when he did, he ran to his daddy every time. He thought maybe he'd just found a way to hurt Michael. Trace was going to suffer where the father could not.

When Grace and Michael retuned Trace got up and walked to his father. He didn't say anything, though Thomas knew he would tell on him later, but the kid did lean over and hug Grace. Thomas was surprised when she hugged the kid back and pulled him onto her chair to sit next to her. Thomas thought maybe it was time for him to get out of here before he hurt someone.

Chapter 8

Ginny watched the people leave the restaurant. She'd been at the big building when Grace Anne had left with the man and was surprised when they both got into the limo and left. She ranted for nearly twenty minutes before she realized she should have followed them to see where they were headed. Lucky for her, she saw the sleek limo parked right across the street from where she'd parked her car.

"You should just bring a gun and shoot her in the head. Then we could get out of this fucking town. It's too...too everything, and I hate it. I want to go back to the house we had in Ohio."

Ginny had gotten better at controlling the others. And they no longer needed a mirror to converse. She could simply hear them now, both Guinevere and Verrie. But Verrie was getting stronger as well. There were times, like last night, when Ginny had no idea what she'd done. It wasn't until she came back that she'd realized that Verrie had killed someone.

"I don't have a gun and, even if I did, don't you think that the other dozen or so people might notice a woman waving one around shooting at her? Guinevere, do you ever think things through or are you forever flying by the seat of your pants? Fuck off and leave me alone." Ginny waited for her to comment again, but she simply faded away. Seconds later she knew why.

"I know damn good and well we have a gun," Verrie said. "I brought it with me when we left. But you're right about shooting her here. Too many witnesses. If we get caught here Cain would probably leave us here to rot."

Ginny didn't comment. All she could think about was Cain. She wanted that man, and badly. She'd gone to him the day before they'd left to get him to give them money to leave and she'd taken one of his shirts. She'd also gotten the private number of Grace Anne.

Ginny had cut the shirt up into small strips and carried pieces of him with her wherever she went. Pulling out the small rectangle now, she buried her nose in it and inhaled. Christ, but the man smelled like sex. She smiled when she thought of what she'd done with a few of the pieces last night. Best climax she'd had in a while.

"Pay attention," Verrie told her with a snap. "See that one over there? The younger one?" Ginny nodded. "He's a looking at them like he wants to kill them. Think we could use him? I mean, it would be easier to get to the little cunt if we could get into that fucking building of hers."

The system that Grace Anne had on her building was tight. And no matter how many times they'd tried to sneak in, someone would catch them and run them off. And that guy with the funny voice had told them that the camera had her picture now so, if anything came up missing, he'd give it to the police. Ginny had left and not returned.

"I know that one. His name is...let me see...Thomas. He's the younger brother of the man. I'm not sure about him. When I was watching the older man the other day, Michael, I could see that that one is a little shit. He goes out of his way to be a prick and he'd be hard to control. And money wouldn't work on him."

Ginny had had Guinevere go to the big building downtown where Michael Cunningham worked and apply for a job. Ginny had seen the way the man had looked at Grace Anne and wondered about it. After they'd gone shopping together and then left for the day Ginny decided to get to Grace Anne through him. Now that they had a little more information on Michael she thought maybe he was going to be more of a problem than any of the other men that had attached themselves to the other girls. Ginny closed her eyes against the frustration of not getting any one of them.

"We just need to kill one of them. And this one seems to be our best bet. She lives here all alone and far enough away from the others that they won't come in and start making our life more difficult." Ginny agreed with Verrie. "Besides, she seems to have done all right for herself. Maybe we could kill this one off and live in her big building before anyone could notice."

That, too, had its merits. The hotel they were staying in was expensive and eating out every day was killing her. She hated that she couldn't just go somewhere and eat; she had to fight with the other two on every choice.

They were quickly running out of funds and she needed to get to her guy in Atlanta soon. He'd been slacking in the money part of their deal. She pulled out her cell phone to call him now, but was distracted watching Michael pull Grace Anne into the limo. Christ, but the man looked at her like she was his last meal and he planned to get his fill. The kid, Trace, was getting into another limo that the older couple got into.

"Looks like someone is going to get lucky tonight," Verrie said sardonically. "I just think there is no accounting for taste for these women. Give me a big man with a lot of push behind his fuck and I'll be a happy woman. Unlike you, who can get off with a couple of fingers and a piece of cotton."

Ginny's anger boiled over the top and she forced pain into Verrie's head. She knew that it would hurt her too. She'd learned that a couple of days ago when she'd tried it on Guinevere. Blood trickled from her nose and she knew that she'd have to pay for this. Verrie was the meanest and the most vindictive of the three of them. She was also quickly becoming the most unstable.

When she was gone Ginny pulled out her phone and called Shawn in Atlanta. He answered on the first ring and he sounded strung out. Great, Ginny thought. He was extremely difficult to try and deal with when he was only just high; this way, he'd be paranoid and mean.

"I need more money. Send me what you have." She didn't like his laughter at her demand. "You think this is funny, dope boy? Well, it's not. How much and how soon?"

"I got myself a little need myself here. And just so's you know, I think I'm not making enough on my cut. I want you to send me more stuff. And the good kind, not that bullshit you sent me the last time either." Ginny nearly hung up and thought about calling him later, but knew that the five thousand they had left wasn't going to last much longer.

"Tell me how much you have and I'll send you the stuff accordingly. And you'll send it today, not when you get the stuff either." She heard him laugh, maniacal and loud. "Are you paying attention to me? I asked you how much?"

"I got you fifty grand. Pretty boy up north is really working hard on trying to impress his new missus. He's got that project, the Madison one, almost finished. We'll have to..." He laughed again and Ginny felt the hair on the back of her neck rise. "We'll have to find us another cow to milk."

This time his laughter was long. She was ready to go to Atlanta and kill the son of a bitch and would have if she had the time. But she needed the little piss ant and knew that, as soon as this was over, she was going to let Verrie have her way with him. She chilled when she heard the other woman agree.

"I'll send it out today," he sang at her. "Today, I'll send it out today. And when I do, you'll send me my drugs, my drugs you'll send to me."

She closed her phone knowing that he'd have to be called back in a few hours to be reminded to send it out again. She hated using such an unreliable source, but in this thing she needed money and he was her easiest source.

~~~

"The money is moving. Daniel got a hit on it about an hour ago and now it's in the system."

Alyssa looked up from her desk as Nathan came into her office.

"It looks like it's our boy Shawn Nicholson. He's been in the program several times over the past five years, all on your tab."

"So, now what? Do you know where the money is going?" She had little knowledge about how this worked and was glad that several months ago her brother had brought Daniel Steward in to talk to her. She'd been both impressed and terrified about what he could do with a computer.

"Daniel said that the tracer he has on the money will lead us to wherever the money goes. Once it stops it'll be up to someone on the other end to figure out where and who picks it up. It will more than likely go to some post office box and, from there, we'll have to sit tight until it's picked up again. Could be soon, but maybe as much as a few weeks; it's hard to tell right now." He pulled her a bottle of water out of the small refrigerator and opened his while she went through the ritual of checking hers for pin holes.

She hated to wait. She wanted this person now. They had taken well over a million dollars over the past eight months and she wanted them caught. But if they wanted to just catch the thief, she'd been told that it could have ended already, but she wanted the one at the other end, the one getting the actual cash.

"Are we paying Daniel for this? I don't want him doing this for us without repaying him. He has spent a great deal of time helping us out." And Alyssa was more than grateful for his discretion too. "Tell him he'll have a job if he wants it when this is over."

Nathan smiled. "He is having a blast, but I'll tell him you insist that he take payment. He told me last week that he'd never had so much fun playing with so much money."

Alyssa looked at her brother sharply and he laughed again.

"No, he's not playing with your money like just ran through your head. He said the only money he likes stealing is his family's. Not other peoples."

Alyssa leaned back in her chair and looked at her brother. He was happy, anyone could see that, but there was more. A lot more. She grinned when he flushed. "Married life must be treating you well, big brother. Is there anything you want to tell me? Something about...I don't know, a baby?" He flushed again. "Oh my God, you are, aren't you?" She stood up and walked around the desk to him.

He stood and hugged her to him. Another baby in the family. How wonderful for them all.

"She wants to tell everyone next weekend," he told her softly. "I've never been so terrified in my life. What if the baby wants to know about me? I mean, I don't exactly have a very good life to tell him about."

"You'll tell him everything. And he'll love you all the more for it. Besides, you turned out just fine. And you're my brother, so you are just perfect the way you are." He laughed and hugged her again. "Does Cain know?"

"No. Just Grace. Jasmine called her first before she even told me. They really are close, aren't they?" Alyssa sat in the chair next to him as he continued. "Grace and Jasmine talk almost daily. I wondered why, but she told me that it was because they were the only singles and they had simply depended on each other when the twins had each other. Weird, if you ask me."

Alyssa had heard Jazzie say that before. That her and Grace had formed their own "twinship" when they'd needed each other. Alyssa guessed that growing up like the Waite children had they would depend on each other more than most children. She knew that Cain felt responsible for all of them all the time.

They talked for a few more minutes before Nathan was called away for another meeting. Alyssa was sitting behind her desk again when a sharp knock at her door was the only thing that warned her she had company. Her son was across the room and into her arms before she had a chance to toss her pen on the desk.

"I thought I'd come here and seduce you, but he insisted on coming to give you a kiss."

She looked up at Cain, her wonderful husband, as he flopped into the chair that Nathan had just left.

"I don't think we're paying the nanny enough. I've been with him for just over two hours and I'm exhausted. I don't know how she does it for the eight hours she has him."

"She makes him mind; you don't. If you'd make him listen to you instead of the other way around, then you'd have more control."

Cain snorted, a nice habit she'd taught him.

"And I know what you're thinking and it isn't the same with me. I let him have his way on some things and you do on everything."

He snorted again. "Yeah, that's why he has every toy known to man and more clothes than he could wear in three childhoods."

"Connor want to have lunch. Connor is hungry."

Alyssa smiled at her son. He'd just picked up the habit of talking about himself in the third person.

"Connor want french fires and catups."

"Okay, but you have to have a sandwich too. How about a grilled cheese with pickles? Or a burger? And if you eat all of the sandwich, I'll let you have a sundae too."

Connor put his finger to his chin and looked like he was thinking it over. Cain laughed, got up, picked him up, and put him on his shoulders. They both seemed to enjoy the trip to the elevator like that. Alyssa was just telling her assistant they were going to the cafeteria when Cain's cell went off. She knew that ring tone and was happy that he didn't answer. His mother could be a real fun-sucker when she called.

"She'll leave a message and, if she doesn't, then that's fine too." He kissed her on the mouth as the doors closed and he leaned in to whisper in her ear. "If I can get Connor to stay with his uncle and aunt tonight, want to have a little fun with the toys I just got?"

Her body reacted like he'd touched her. She could feel her pussy get wet and swell. She nodded at him, afraid she'd be begging him to take her right now rather than wait until they got home. She leaned back against the wall of the elevator and looked at him.

His growl made her shudder. "You keep looking at me like that and I'll stop the first person I see and ask them to watch our son while I take you back up to your office and ravage you."

"Okay," she told him, and laughed when he growled again. "I think that the aunt and uncle thing is a great idea. We have that charity thing to go to tonight, but I'm pretty sure that between the time we get home and when we have to leave I can make you very…relaxed."

"Deal. I'll see if I can drop Connor off after lunch, then I'll come back here and we'll get a start on that plan." He adjusted his cock and made her body heat. "Maybe I could skip lunch and just have you."

"No. Connor hungry. Want grilled cheese and french fries then Connor want to play on swinger."

"Its swing, little buddy," Drew said as the doors opened on the ground floor. He ruffled Connor's hair as he looked at them "I'm glad to see you two. There's a problem with one of the buildings on Tenth. We have a few people wanting us to change the venue for the building and they are sick of me telling them no. Wanna handle this one?"

He grinned at her and she knew she wasn't going to like this. "What exactly are we using the building for that has them all up in arms? And don't we already own that entire block?"

He nodded.

"So what the hell are they bitching about now?"

"We're using it for storage at the moment. And they don't like the fact that you're making the other blocks surrounding you look bad because of the improvements you're making on that one. They seemed to think you're trying to outdo them."

Alyssa rolled her eyes. "Of all the stupid... Set up some sort of improvement loans program. Make the interest low, but not stupidly. Have Nathan work with you on it; he's been working on something similar on the Madison Project. Oh, by the way, there was movement on the money. Nathan came by just before Connor and Cain did."

They were being seated in the large cafeteria and Drew joined them. "I know. I was tied up with the committee on 'let's be ignorant' when the call came in. These people who are bitching, most of them are the same ones you bought the building from in the first place. Are you sure you want to lend them money now? They didn't strike me as all that good with their money in the first place."

"They have to put their buildings up for collateral. That way, it's a win-win for us if they fail again." Cain said this as he buckled

Connor in the seat. She was laughing when he turned to them. "What? I think it's a good idea."

"It is. I just didn't think you were that ruthless." She turned to Drew again. "Put that in the loan agreement. Now, no more business. I'm hungry too."

Chapter 9

Grace sat across from Michael as they rode across town. He said he wanted to take her home and she couldn't think of a single reason why he couldn't. But she'd thought that Trace would be with them and he'd gone home with his grandparents instead. She wasn't happy with the turn of events.

"You're upset," he said to her after a few minutes. "I didn't tell Trace to go with them. I think my mother invited him to go and what little boy doesn't want to spend time with their loving grandparents?"

She didn't answer because she had no idea what kids did with grandparents. She didn't know hers and she was pretty sure that her parents wouldn't have let them go to stay with them anyway. There was too much they could have told them.

"Grace, come over here and kiss me."

She glared at him and didn't move.

"Okay, I'll come to you."

He slid across the expanse of the seat and sat beside her. Before she could react, she was straddling his lap and he was tugging at the zipper at the side of her dress. She grabbed a handful of his hair and yanked hard to stop him.

"Now that I have your attention," she told him with another hard tug. "I want you to stop doing whatever you're doing. I'm not going to sleep with you again and that's final. Buy my building so that I can move on. I have too much at stake for you to be—"

She was suddenly on her back and he was over her. As he ran his hand up her thigh and under her dress she knew that she'd lost control and tried to think how to roll him off her and get out without him making her crazier with need for him.

"You're very beautiful when you're angry, did you know that?" he asked her as he moved his mouth along the column of her throat. "And when you're pissed as you are now, all I can think about is how much I want to have you surrender to me, how quickly I can be inside of you."

"Let me go, Michael. This isn't happening." She knew she was lying the moment the words left her mouth. "Get off me. You can't keep doing this to me."

"Yes, I can. You know it." His hand was on her bare hip and, when he reached around and cupped her ass, she moaned. "You're so responsive to me. My cock aches to be deep inside of you again. If you come for me I'll make it worth your while."

She thought she could gladly come with just the sound of his voice. He was moving his hand along her thigh again as he rocked between her legs. She wrapped herself around him as he slid his finger under her panties and into her soft folds.

"You are wet. And hot. I want to drink from you, Grace. Let me taste you when you come. Then I want to fuck this luscious pussy until you come again and again." He pulled away, opened his pants, and his cock sprang free. "See what you do to me? Christ, I've been hard since I came inside of you earlier."

Licking her lips, Grace leaned up and wrapped her hand around him. He was hard and velvety soft. His cock was hot and smooth and there was a pearled drop of his cum just on the tip that she needed to taste. Leaning into him, she ran her tongue over his purple crown and gathered it into her mouth.

His hiss of approval made her adjust herself so that she could take him into her mouth. She had a moment of wondering why this man could make her want things she knew she shouldn't when he laced his fingers in her hair and pulled her to his cock.

"Suck me, Grace. Suck on my cock until I can't stand it any longer."

She took him into her mouth and moaned.

"Christ."

She wasn't comfortable sitting the way she was, but found she really didn't care. She ran her tongue along his length and cupped his balls in her fingers. The salty taste of him made her want more, but stopping what she was doing wasn't an option right now. She was enjoying herself too much. When he pulled her head back by her hair she tried to go back to his lovely cock, but he pulled her again.

"I want to be inside of you. Right now. I want to fuck you and fill you with my cum." She moved back from him, but not before she took him into her mouth again. "Christ, you're killing me."

She lay back as he pulled her dress over her hips. Her panties, soaked through, were no match for him and she heard them tear. She closed her eyes to try and get control. She was so close.

When he didn't move, didn't take her, she looked up at him. He had the most beautiful face, she thought suddenly, and reached up to touch him. He kissed her hand as she ran it along his cheek. He looked at her as he slowly filled her.

She wanted to close her eyes again. Even as he rocked into her slowly she knew that things were never going to be the same. He was taking something right now and she couldn't for the life of her take it back. Her heart was his. Even after such a short time together, she knew without a doubt that this man, over all the other men she'd known, was going to be more than just someone she had dinner with and maybe on occasion slept with. The handful of men she'd allowed in her bed was nothing to this one.

"Michael, please. I need you to take me." She knew that what she was saying was more than just a simple fucking; she actually wanted him to take her. And that terrified her more than the thought of her mother and her threats.

Leaning down, he took her mouth. The kiss was gentle yet hungry, soft but thorough. He was making her heart pound and her blood boil all while he was breaking her in two.

"Come for me, Grace. Come with me now."

Her body reacted to his command immediately. She bowed up beneath him as he filled her. She felt his teeth sink into her neck, the hard bite of possession. Even as she came again from the short pain, she knew that she had to get away from him as soon as possible, before it was too late.

As he dropped onto her then rolled, taking her with him onto the soft leather seat, she thought maybe it was too late for either of them. She felt the tears fill her eyes and wondered why now? Why now, after all this time, did a man come into her life when she had to leave him to save him?

~~~

Michael felt her tears, but didn't comment on them. He wondered if he'd hurt her, but knew enough to know that the tears splashing on his chest had nothing to do with that. She'd changed; right before his eyes, she'd become more to him. Michael closed his eyes to the sudden terror he felt. The terror of knowing that Grace Waite was more than just a simple lay in the back of the limo. She was becoming more.

He held her until she started to stir. He let her go and watched her sit up and try to adjust her clothing. He grinned when she held up her panties to him and laughed when she tossed them at him.

"Those are a one of a kind, you know. I have no idea how much they sell for, but those particular panties were going to be featured in the next catalogue and now I'll have to remake them. I hope you're satisfied." She sat on the seat and tried to run her fingers through her hair. "We can't do this again."

He didn't say anything, knowing that, as soon as he got her to his house, it was indeed going to happen again. Only, this time, he was going to take her to his bed, not against the wall or the floor of a limo.

"Where are we going anyway? I thought you were taking me home." She looked out the dark window and turned to him again. "Where are we?"

He reached for his pants before answering. Christ, she was going to be pissed. "I'm taking you to my house. You said that you

74

were tired, and so am I. Frankly, I don't think you and I could fit in your bed and do all the things I want to do to you in it."

"Your home." She said it so hard he looked up at her as he buckled his belt. "I told you I wanted to go to my house. That was where you said you were taking me. Turn this thing around right now and take me back to my house."

He reached over and pulled her across his lap. His cock stirred beneath her and he knew she'd felt it. She looked at him wide-eyed and he kissed her mouth quickly.

"Sit still and maybe he'll behave." She tried to get off his lap, but he was stronger and he held her still. "I mean it, Grace. If you don't stop squirming around I'm going to have to throw you down again and lick that luscious pussy of yours. I've not had the opportunity to taste you yet and I'm dying to do so."

She looked so hurt he almost let her go. "Why?" she asked him quietly, and he knew she was asking for more than just why he wanted her again.

"I don't know. You're beautiful, but it's more than that. You're brilliant and fun to be with; you make me laugh, and you make me harder than any other woman I know. But why do I want you? I really don't know." He pulled her head to his shoulder and she let him. "Grace, please come home with me. I want to make love to you properly in a bed this time. And then in the morning, if we haven't killed each other, we'll talk."

"I'm not going to stay, Michael. I have to leave before they find you. If they do, you've no idea what they'll do to you. They're evil and they're...I can't let anything like I know they're capable of doing be done to you."

He held her tighter. The thought of letting her go making him panicky. He didn't understand it, but knew that if he let this woman get away from him that things, especially his life, would never be the same.

"We'll talk tomorrow. Tonight, we're going to make love, eat, make love and then, if we have the strength, make love again." Her giggle made him smile. "I'll even make you breakfast in bed if you don't kill me first."

"Okay. But tomorrow, we go back to our original plan. You buy the building and I move on. I have enough things to worry about without you making things more complicated."

He nodded, not agreeing with her, but knowing that things were going to get really complicated and soon.

She laid in his arms the rest of the way to his house. They both must have fallen asleep because, when he opened his eyes, he realized they had stopped. He gently shook her awake and stretched when she slid to the other side of the seats. She looked good enough to eat all rumpled and sexy and he wanted her again, much to his amazement.

He reached for the door just as it was being opened. He grinned and wondered if the driver, Wells, had been listening for them to wake or if he was that good. As soon as Michael was out, he reached in for Grace. He looked over at Wells and winked as she stood beside him.

"Wells, my good man, I'd like you to meet Miss Grace Waite. Grace, this is my good friend, butler, and all around handy man, Timothy Wells. He's been with my family for nearly fifty years."

Wells took her hand and kissed it. "Good to meet you, miss. You and the boss here, you sure do make a very fine-looking couple. You two look like you could be models for them cake toppers at weddings." He shook Michael's hand before continuing. "Master Trace called, sir, and he said that he wanted me to fetch him home first thing in the morning. He said you promised him blueberry pancakes and sausage links. If you want, I can have him here around ten if you and Miss Waite will be ready for him by then."

Grace buried her face in his shoulder and he lifted her face to his. He kissed her on the mouth as he turned to Wells. He didn't want her to be ashamed that the household knew she was spending the night. "Ten will be fine. And please, have your wife make some bacon too." Michael turned to Grace. "What do you want extra? Molly can make the best pancakes in the world and they're so fluffy they need the blueberries in them to keep them on the plate."

She looked at Wells. "I'm not a big fan of pancakes, but I'll try hers. And blueberries are my favorite. Tell your wife I look forward to trying them."

They walked into the house and he showed her around. The house had been a real buy and the timing couldn't have been more perfect. He'd gotten such a good deal on the house and the surrounding twenty acres that he'd had an office put in just so he could stay here some days instead of traveling to the city every day.

The front hall was the perfect place to start. The double wide staircase went up the first level and split off into two different directions. The stairs to the left led to the guest bedrooms and the one to the right to the family's rooms. He bypassed the stairs in favor of the lower level, knowing that if he got her upstairs he'd never come back down again tonight.

"This room is what Molly calls the sitting room. I like it. It's warm and if I want to have a fire, it's easy to flip on the gas. And if you pull this wall away." Michael reached over and moved the panel that slid into the wall beside it. "You can watch a little television or listen to the sound system. Trace and I spend a lot of time in here."

"I can see why. It's the kind of room you can kick off your shoes and lay back." She wandered over to the set of windows that bracketed each side of the fireplace. "The view is amazing. I didn't even know there were these kinds of places in New York."

He sat in the overstuffed chair near the fireplace before saying anything. "It's the reason we loved it so much. Trace wanted a yard like his grandma and I wanted the privacy that being out in the middle of nowhere could give you."

She moved to the other door and into the dining room. He got up to follow her after kicking off his shoes. He knew he should pick them up, but was loath to leave her to discover his house on his own. She was talking to Molly when he entered.

"Oh no, miss, it's no problem. I love to bake and having some reason to do so makes my day. Tim, he doesn't appreciate a good baked bread, but the mister here does." Michael walked up behind Grace as Molly continued. "The miss here was telling me that she liked the smell of my bread. I was telling her that I could make her blueberry muffins in the morning while you and young Trace have your pancakes. She was fussing at me not to do so."

"Blueberry muffins with the sugar on top? Oh, Grace, you'll have to have them. They're only rivaled by her apple crunch. I hope you'll bake enough for me to take to work on Monday." Molly nodded and disappeared in the kitchen. He turned Grace in his arms and looked down at her. "She'll make them anyway so you might as well decide to eat them now. You wouldn't want to hurt her feelings now, would you?"

She glared at him. "Do you always get your way? I mean, it seems like you think you should so I'm wondering if you do. I'm not a pushover, Mr. Cunningham, so you'd better get that thought out of your head right now."

"Are you hungry?" he asked her suddenly. "Do you think you could wait for, I don't know…a couple of hours before you'll need to eat again?"

"I suppose so, why?" He scooped her up into his arms and headed for the stairs. "What is wrong with you? Put me down this instant. Of all the—Michael Cunningham, put me down."

He stopped halfway up the right flank of stairs and put her on her feet. He was glad for the wall behind her because, when he pulled her to him and rocked into her, she leaned back against it and lifted her leg over his hip. Lifting her up by her ass, he was glad when she wrapped both her legs around him so that he could walk and feel her pussy pressed over his raging hard-on. If he made it till morning he was going to be really surprised.

And if they made it downstairs again before ten, it was going to be a miracle.

Chapter 10

Thomas sat in the lobby and waited for Michael to come in. He looked at his watch again and couldn't believe his stepbrother was coming in so late. It was nearly eight-thirty on Monday morning and he still wasn't in. Thomas just knew it had something to do with that girl.

He thought about the woman who had approached him Sunday afternoon. How she'd gotten his name and address was still a little fuzzy to him, but he liked her idea about getting back at Michael. He smiled when he thought of her plan.

"You bring me the man and I'll let you do whatever you want to him after I get the girl. She's all I want anyway. After that, I could care less what you do."

He nodded and knew that for whatever he thought of doing to Michael to get back at him, this woman could do worse to him. He sat back on his chair and looked at her. "And what is it that you expect me to do with him? You must know that he's my brother. And what is it you want the girl for anyway? I might want to fuck her instead of giving her to you." Thomas stroked his cock. "She and I had a connection at dinner on Friday. I think I might want to pursue it."

She looked at him strangely before answering. "All right. You can fuck her, but she's still mine. When you've had your fun, then I take her away and you will have your stepbrother. I know all about your relationship with him. You should be more discreet when you two have a fight. The underlings talk a lot."

So here he was trying to make nice with his stepbrother and get closer to him. Thomas thought about using Trace as bait, but didn't want to have to convince the kid to come with him. Trace hadn't trusted him almost from birth; another reason to hate his stepbrother, for making his nephew hate him.

When Michael finally came into the building at nine-fifteen Thomas had been about ready to leave. He was just standing up to do so when he spotted him coming down the main lobby. He walked toward him and tried not to look like he felt—like he wanted to murder him right now.

"I need to talk to you. It's about working for you again."

Michael didn't stop moving toward the elevators as he answered, "no."

"Please. I need to have a job or my parole officer gets to put one of those ankle things on me. And that shit just isn't going to set well with what I have planned."

Thomas stepped into the elevator as soon as Michael did. "Well, you should have thought of that before you fucked the girl on her desk. It may not seem like much to you, but I do have a reputation to uphold."

Thomas wanted to pull out the knife he'd purchased this morning and plunge it into his heart. How dare he to talk down to him as if he were better than him. Thomas took several deep breaths as he tried to regain control of his temper. He counted to ten, then again before he spoke, but by then the elevator had stopped on the upper floor and Michael we getting out.

"You have to give me another chance. I promise I'll try and not screw up again. You have to give me something here, Michael. I don't want to go back to jail."

Jail had been some place he'd never go again, even if he had to shoot a couple of cops to do it. It was a place that he'd been low man on the food chain and not a place he liked. Thomas shuddered as he thought about the person who had introduced him to being a "girlfriend." Thomas caught up with Michael, trying to outrun the memories. The man, Jack, had taught him a great deal about submission and what happened to his "girlfriend" if he didn't.

"Look, I don't have the energy to fuck with you today," Michael said as he hung up his jacket. "You come back tomorrow and I'll see what I can do. I'm not making any promises, but I'll see."

Thomas wanted to tell him to go and fuck himself, but knew that he'd never get the job if he did. Instead, he thanked him and walked out of his office and down the hall to the elevator. He was just stepping inside when he saw Trace. The boy was coming toward him at full tilt and stepped in the elevator before it closed. He was sure the kid was going to regret it the moment he realized who was with him.

"Why aren't you in school?" Thomas asked him when he saw his nephew practically became one with the wall. "I thought all you brainiacs spent, like, all your free time there."

"Its spring break. I don't have to be back until the Monday after next. Dad and I are taking a trip this week. What are you doing here? How come you aren't in jail again?"

Thomas lunged for the boy just as the elevator opened. Trace darted out just as several people stepped in. Thomas got out just as the door was closing and went after him. The smart-assed kid was going to pay for that comment, and he was going to make sure that he paid dearly. The kid took off out of the building just as Thomas did and he was darting down the street. He followed for about four blocks, losing him twice before he couldn't find him. He was just about to go back when he saw him go into a big building and close the door. He started to follow, but when he got to the building the intercom wouldn't work and he stood out there for several minutes pounding on the door that no one would answer. Thomas looked around. Maybe he'd gotten the wrong building and he started to go down to the next one. By the time he'd moved down three more he was exhausted.

Thomas was going to get the kid if it was the last thing he did. The fucking little bastard would probably tell his dad some stupid lie and Thomas would not only be out of a job, but he'd also be barred from the building again. Pulling out his phone he called his dad.

"I just saw Trace leaving the Cunningham building. I was worried he'd be hurt so, when I went after him, he took off. I can't stand that he thinks I'm going to hurt him all the time. Would you call Michael and make him aware that his son is out running around again?" Thomas groaned when he realized he should have called his mother first. She would have maybe believed him quicker than his dad.

"What did you do to make him run, Thomas? If you hurt that boy, you and I are going to tangle and then Michael will—"

"I didn't hurt him. And I didn't make him run. I told you, he was leaving the building and I followed. I lost him on the street." Thomas had one more thing to add to his list of grievances from his stepbrother. "I would have called Michael but, like you, he would have blamed me. You know I could have just let him run wild in the streets, but I called to let someone know."

His father relented, but still didn't act as if he believed him. His dad said he'd let Michael know as soon as he hung up. And Thomas hung up soon after. He watched the three buildings and when no one came out after thirty minutes, he moved on. Fucking kid would probably end up dead and then what fun could Thomas have? He was grinning when he went back to his apartment. Time to make some arrangements.

~~~

"Your father said for you to wait here until he comes out of his meetings. He said to tell you to behave yourself and not to touch anything." Grace sat down at the big desk as she spoke to him. "I don't know why parents tell their kids that. How are you supposed to know things if you can't touch them?"

Trace grinned as he stuffed the rest of the grapes in his mouth. He was glad the door downstairs hadn't been locked. He was sure that Uncle Thomas would have hurt him if he had been able to catch him. Trace took a big drink of his water before he spoke. "Thanks again, Miss Grace. I was all turned around until I saw your building. I'm glad that man downstairs didn't get mad when I almost knocked him over." He watched her face to see if she was mad. She didn't appear to be, so he relaxed a little.

He didn't tell her the real reason he'd been running around. He was sure she'd never believe him and was afraid she'd make him go back with his uncle again. Trace looked down at his scuffed shoes before he looked up at Grace when she started talking. He liked her. He liked her a whole lot. She didn't talk to him like he was a kid and she always had something for him to snack on.

"Arnold. He's my friend and a pain in my ass." She picked up this sheet of paper with a lot of small pictures on it. "See this? It's called a contact sheet. I'm supposed to pick one picture out of all these to put on the cover of my catalogue. Why on earth would you need..." He could see her counting. "Fifty-three? He took fifty-three pictures? Christ, why did I... Anyway, he took all these pictures and I'm supposed to pick the best one."

Trace looked around the little room. It looked like someone had taken a bunch of crayons, melted them down, and poured them all over the walls. He thought maybe it would be something that had to grow on you, as his grandma said, but he wasn't sure why anyone would want it to. So far as he knew, some of those colors just looked gross together. He looked back at Grace when she cleared her throat.

"You don't like it, do you?"

He started to nod then shook his head. He didn't want to hurt her feelings, but it was really bad.

"I don't either most of the time. But it's here to remind me of what I came from."

"You came from a weird house if that's how they painted your walls, Miss Grace. It's sort of sickening."

He flushed and she laughed before she answered him. "It's not paint, Trace, but material. It's all the material scraps that I had with me when I finally had enough money to buy this building. See, I started out just using the leftover pieces to make my designs. I would stay up late at night and sew these small dresses and then think about ways to improve them. Every day I would learn a little more until I was able to present my first design to the previous owner. He loved it and promised me that he'd take it to the next show. He even let me help with the larger design of the dress. It's that one over there."

Trace got up and walked to where she pointed. There was a mannequin behind a glass wall and she was dressed in a pretty black and purple dress. Trace didn't know anything about clothes and less about fashion. If it fit when he tried it on, he figured he looked good. Besides, his dad would have told him if he looked dorky.

"You made this?" He looked back at her when she said yes. "It's nice. Nothing I think my aunts would wear, but I like it. I bet it looked pretty on you."

"You're very kind, and I did wear it. Phillip told me if I wore it on the floor and sold more than a hundred copies of it, he'd take me on as his apprentice."

Trace looked at the dress again and tried to remember if he'd seen anyone wearing one like it. He couldn't, but then he didn't know all that many women. He looked back at her and decided that she'd not sold any if the dopey look on her face was any indication.

"I'm sorry, Miss Grace. I guess you had to work really hard the next time, huh? Is that why you only make underwear here now?"

She grinned at him before answering. "I sold over ten thousand units, Trace. More than any other design he had. And I thought he'd just kick me out of the place, but he said a promise was a promise and helped me design my label." She stood up and handed him the picture next to the dress. "That's a copy of the first order we filled. And the amount. I was surprised that he charged so much." She picked up a magazine next to his chair. "And this is my catalogue that comes out this summer. See the underwear, as you call them? They're our number one sellers. Pretty underwear is what women want to wear."

Trace handed her back the catalogue and looked over at the wall again. "You put those scraps on the wall to remind you of the pieces you had to put together in order to make it big then?"

"Very good. Yes, that's right." She ruffled his hair and he hugged her. "Not many people get it so quickly if at all."

He was watching a "set" be put together when he noticed the puppy. It was sitting in the corner all scrunched up in a ball and Trace made his way to it. He was just kneeling down to touch it when one of the men nailing something together came over.

"We been trying to catch him all day. He musta got in when we was bringing in the lumber. Pick him up, will ya, and toss him in the back? His mom will come and get him, or, if she's been hit, then he'll have to fend for himself."

The puppy whimpered when Trace touched him. He was hurt, probably from this guy. Trace bundled him up in his arms and went to find a place to hide him so that when his dad came to get him they could take him somewhere safe. Grace was coming toward him with a frown and he was afraid she was going to tell him to do what the guy had done.

"I won't throw him outside. It's raining and he'll get a cold. There isn't any reason for you to be cruel to a little puppy." He brushed at the tear on his face and turned away before she could make fun of him like his uncle did.

"You feel better for lashing out at me, or did you want me to kick the dog so you can at least feel justified for snapping at me like that?"

He turned to look at her angry face.

"I was going to suggest we take him to the vet just down the block, but I can see you have it under control."

She started to walk away and he said her name. "I'm sorry. I just...I love animals. And that guy over there wanted me to throw him out back to fend for himself. Could we really take him to the vet?"

She told her assistant Becky to get rid of the man who had wanted to toss out the dog and told her to make sure that everyone left at five. She grabbed up her coat and they were out the door and into a cab in no time. Trace looked over at the woman seated next to him

"You're not like the other women my dad sometimes dates." She snorted and he smiled. "You do that too. The pretty women that dad used to date wouldn't do that if you paid them a million bucks. But you don't care, do you?"

"I most certainly do not. And for the record, I'm not seeing your dad. He and I have an arrangement. He's going to buy the building and I'm going to disappear."

That made the area around his heart hurt a bit. He didn't want her to disappear; he really liked Miss Grace. He was trying to think of a way to make her want to stick around for a little while longer when her phone rang. He watched her answer it.

She was already a very pale woman, he noticed. He thought her skin looked like milk and was really smooth like it too. He thought of her as the most beautiful woman he'd ever seen and thought maybe his dad did too. But as soon as she put the phone to her ear she seemed to get paler. He watched her close the phone with shaky hands and put it back into her pocket. He didn't know a great deal about adults and less about what made them scared, but he'd bet his brand new bed that someone had scared the crap out of Miss Grace.

Trace did the only thing he could think of and he reached out and took her hand. She took it and held it really tight. She seemed to be so sad all of a sudden when she looked at him and he decided right then and there that he loved Miss Grace.

"I'm really going to miss you, Trace. It's been a pleasure knowing you."

As soon as they got to the vet he called his dad.

Chapter 11

Michael answered his phone on the first ring. He was right in the middle of the biggest deal in his career and he didn't have time for calls.

"Whatever you want, you'll have to call back later. I'm too fucking busy to talk to you right now." The silence at the other end had him close his eyes. He just knew it was going to be his mother. When Trace spoke, his heart started to pound.

"Dad, I'm sorry, but I found him and they wanted to throw him in the back to die and I didn't know she was going to let me take care of him, but I was mean to her and then she got this phone call and whoever it was made her sad, then she held my hand and told me that she was going to miss me."

Michael could hear the tears in his son's voice and took a deep breath. "Okay, son, let's start over. Who did you find and who wanted to throw them out to die?"

Seemed a reasonable place to start, but apparently not to his son. "She's going to leave us. Are you going to let her go? I love her, Dad, and I don't want her to go away."

He figured he was talking about Grace, but wanted to be sure. "You mean Grace? She's not going anywhere, Trace. She and I are working on a deal that will give her a better place to work and I'll have—"

87

"You're not listening to me. She got this phone call and I think that person…hang on, the doctor wants to ask me a question."

Michael stood up. His son was at a doctor's office. He grabbed his coat to go to him when he realized he had no idea where he was. The last he'd heard he was with Grace. He sat down hard, thinking something had happened to her. When Trace came back on the line, Michael was ready to scream.

"They wanted a name to call him. I hope you don't mind, but I'm calling him Walter. They said he need a good name and Grace said I should add something distinguished to it. So his name is Walter Stuffinpuppy the Fourth. Is that okay with you?"

Michael laid his head on his desk. "That's fine, son. Where are you?"

"At the vet."

Michael waited for more, but apparently he was waiting in vain. "And you're there with Grace and Walter?" Again, a short, to the point answer. "Can I speak to Grace, you think? Or can Walter come to the phone?" At this point, he would talk to anyone to figure out what was going on. His son's laughter caught him off guard.

"Walter is a dog, Dad. Grace is out in the lobby with my coat. I left her my stuff so she couldn't leave me. She said she was going to have to leave us, Dad. I don't want her to."

Neither did Michael. He stood again and walked toward the door. "What vet are you at and I'll come and get you both…well, all three. And then we'll talk about Walter and his new owner." Trace giggled again. "I'm assuming you're his new owner, right?"

"Yeah. I couldn't let them throw him outside in the rain, Dad, and the vet says that he'd got a cold and needs some TLC. I had to ask him what that meant and I've got plenty of tender loving care for him, I promise."

Michael didn't doubt it. "Does Grace know that you called me?" At his son's 'no' he grinned. "Don't tell her. She and I will have a long talk when I get there. And son."

"Yeah, Dad?"

Michael grinned bigger when he heard the suspicion in his son's voice. "If Walter isn't house trained, you're cleaning up his messes."

Michael called his mom next. "Can you call Markus for me and tell them we'll have to meet tomorrow? I have something to do and it can't wait any longer."

"Yes. I'll call him now. Is there anything wrong? It's not the deal, is it? Oh Michael, tell me what I can do to fix it."

He pushed the button to the elevator to go down to his car. "No, nothing to do with that. It's Grace and Trace." He liked the sound of that. "Trace apparently found a dog and someone he loves more than me."

"He doesn't love a dog more than you. He may say that, but he doesn't. I remember once when you claimed to love the lady across the hall from us more than ice cream. It didn't last. The next time I went to the store and got you your favorite, Miss Too-tight-dress was history."

Michael laughed. "If I remember correctly, I only loved her for her cookies. Back then I don't think I would have noticed how tight her dress was. No, it's Grace. She told him she was leaving and he's decided that he loves her too much to let her go."

His mom snorted. "Well, at least one of you is smart enough to know a good woman when he sees one. Tell Trace that his grandmother thinks he's the smarter of the two of you and I'm rooting for him."

Michael was still smiling when he pulled up in front of the Main Paws Veterinary twenty minutes later. He stepped inside just in time to hear a shrill whistle and a little boy crying.

Before he could step in and fix it Grace started barking orders like a drill sergeant. "You, I want you to stop yelling at the top of your lungs and sit still. You're making matters worse by caterwauling like a cat with his tail under a rocker."

The woman with the furry piece of fluff in her hands stopped shouting. Grace turned to the nurse standing there and started on her. "Take that…what the hell is that anyway?"

"It's a gecko, miss. And I don't appreciate you taking over like you own the place. The doctor will be—"

"Happier if he doesn't have to bail you out of jail for causing a riot. Take that lizard in the back and see if it needs stitches. Why you don't have a leash law in here is beyond me." Grace turned to the little boy who was sobbing in his mother's lap. "You should be whipped. And don't you dare try to tell me that you didn't throw that cat on top of the gecko on purpose. I saw you. And if he needs therapy after this, I'm going to make sure you get the bills. Poor thing will probably lose all his scales by the next full moon."

"I don't believe gecko have scales, honey," Michael said to her when she looked at him. "And therapy? The poor thing will probably need years of it when this is over."

"He called you," she said with a glare, and he nodded. "Why? No, don't tell me, he thought that you'd not turn him down bringing the puppy home if he could show you that he was injured. Well, he's fine. He needs a good home and if you can't provide it for him, I'll take him to my nephew. Connor will love him."

Michael wanted to pull her to him and kiss her senseless, but thought she'd hit him. And as much as he wanted her right now, he didn't want her to hurt him in front of a room full of witnesses. He braced his arms over his chest so he couldn't touch her and smiled. "He can keep the dog. I've wanted to get him one for weeks now. As for your nephew, I'd love to meet him." He stepped closer, unable to help himself. "You are the reason I'm here."

~~~

Grace tried to get out of going back to his house with him after they left the vet. Trace was so happy about getting to keep the little dog that she'd let her better judgment get away from her. She was in his limo again and speeding across town in less time than she could have arranged it.

"I'm going to have to have a cab take me back home tonight, so will you lend me enough money to pay for the ride?"

Michael simply grinned.

"I have an early meeting in the morning so I have to leave by eight to get back in time to get to bed early."

"I'll make sure you get back in time for your meeting tomorrow. I have a meeting too and we can share the ride in." He leaned back on the seat, entirely too full of himself. "You should bring some clothes to leave at the house so you can have something to change into when you're here."

"I'm not spending the night. I told you, we can't see each other anymore. You need to purchase the building so that I can get on with my life." She looked over at Trace and realized he'd fallen asleep. "You can't keep coming around like you're...like we're seeing each other."

"But we are. A lot less than I would like, but we are seeing each other." He pulled her to him. "Like right now, for example. I'd very much like to see what you have on under this pretty blouse. Are you wearing one of those skimpy little pieces of lace like you had on this weekend?"

Her body seemed to have a mind of its own where he was concerned. While she was trying to tell it to back off and stop it, it was leaning over him and running its hands through his hair. She tried to tell her mouth to back the fuck up, but it was covering his with its own. Grace moaned when he cupped her breast in his hand.

"I want you, Grace. I think about all the things I want to do to you and where, and now that I have you right here I can't decide where to begin." She moaned again when he pinched her nipple. "You want me too, admit it. You'd like nothing better than to have me pull you into my lap and suckle at your lovely nipple. Christ, I want you so bad."

She tried again to pull back, but he wouldn't let her. "Michael, I have to leave soon. You're not safe with me around you. They will hurt you both if you keep this up."

He pulled her to his lap and opened her blouse. She had a moment to wonder about his son sleeping now two feet away, but he had her breast free and in his mouth immediately.

Her entire body tightened. She knew that, without much thought, she could gladly let him fuck her right now. He let go of her nipple with a small pop and looked up at her. She was panting hard and she could feel his cock as he rocked up into her.

"Come home with me, Grace. Spend the night with me and I promise you'll not regret it," he begged her.

She looked down at him and his need. She brushed her hand over his face. "It's not going to last. I have to leave and make you both safe. They're going to get me."

"I can keep you safe. I want to keep you safe. I'm...I'm falling in love with you, and I know that Trace is ready to claim you if I don't. Stay with me, let me help you. I swear you'll be safe."

She pulled her blouse down and sat in the seat. She looked over at Trace and then back at Michael. "There are things...people you have to know about before..." She looked away from him. "You might want to change your mind after I tell you everything."

He pulled her face back to his and lifted her chin so that she could look him in the eye. "Whatever it is, whoever is trying to hurt you, together we can take care of it. I love you, Grace. I've never said that to a woman before, but I do."

"Oh Michael, why now? I love you as well, but our timing sucks." They made the rest of the ride in silence. She wanted to start as soon as they reached his house, but there was dinner to make and then Trace needed to find a place to put his new pet. Walter didn't seem to mind being put in the boy's bed and Trace was happy, so things settled very quickly.

She was putting the dishes in the dishwasher when Molly came in with the last of the things from the dining room. Grace turned to her when she heard her enter the room and was uncomfortable all of a sudden.

"I don't know if I did it right. I usually just throw away whatever takeout I've eaten from and go to bed."

Molly continued to stare.

"I thought that you'd want the leftovers put...have I done something wrong?"

"No, miss. It's just that...I don't think I've ever had the lady of the house help me before. It's just that I expected...well, I guess I expected you to be like the others." Molly took the dishtowel from her and put it on the sink. "You're not a thing like the others and you just don't care either, do you, miss?"

"First, I'm not the lady of the house. I'm a guest and nothing more. If you want to know the truth, I'm not even sure how I came to be here tonight. And please stop calling me 'miss.' I have no idea why it creeps me out so much, but I'd very much like for you to call me Grace or Grace Anne. As for the others? I'm not sure what sort of people you worked for before, but if they didn't help you out when they brought home unexpected guests then shame on them." Grace took the last of the leftovers and shoved them in the refrigerator. "Molly, what am I going to do?"

Grace could feel the tears threaten. She didn't know why she was so upset, but she had an idea that it was because she liked being here too much. She loved having Trace come to her when he had a problem, and she was in love with Michael. Things were moving much too fast and she wasn't sure if she wanted it to slow down so she could savor it or just speed on by so she could leave before it was too late.

"Do you love them, mi…Grace? The men, do you love them?" Grace nodded at Molly's question. "Then there you have it. There is no problem that love can't fix. You just have to trust him. Michael is a good man, a bit on the stubborn side, but a good man. Aren't you, sir?"

Grace turned to find Michael standing in the doorway looking at her. She felt his love pour over her and she wanted more than anything to do just way Molly had suggested. He stood and came toward her as he spoke.

"Thanks, Molly. And yes, I'm a bit stubborn, but not near as stubborn as some designers I know." He stood in front of her and pulled her into his arms. "Trace wants you to come and tuck him in. He said he's never had a person who wasn't related to him do it before."

They walked up the stairs together holding hands. Grace knew that they were going to talk and she also knew that what she was about to tell him would either be the end of what could have been or the beginning of his worst nightmare.

93

"My mother has split personalities," she told him as soon as his door was closed. "And she murdered at least one man while I was still living at home."

Chapter 12

Cain looked down at the file in front of him then back up at Drew. Payton was pacing the room and neither man was saying anything. They were waiting on Alyssa to come back from the meeting. Cain started to pick it up again, but couldn't bring himself to touch it. It was just too…too much.

"I'm sorry I'm late. I have… What is it? What's happened now?" Alyssa came to sit near him at the conference table. "Cain? Tell me."

"The money," he started, and then cleared his throat. "The missing money has been traced to my mother. And she may be in New York."

"Oh my God, Grace. We have to call her—what the fuck are you two doing standing there? Go and get her and bring her back here right fucking now." Alyssa stood up, started toward the other two men, and Cain pulled her back.

"We can't. Not yet at any rate. We need…" Drew looked at Payton before he continued. "He has a plan to catch her in the act. We think she might have been the person all along trying to murder all of us."

That was the hardest thing to get his mind wrapped around. His mother was a murderer. He thought about all the things she'd been up to, the way she'd been—

"If they catch her in the act of no more than just stealing from you then all she'll get is a slap on the wrist. If we catch her at trying to get to Gr—"

Alyssa cut Payton off. "If you even whisper the words, 'I'm going to use Grace as bait,' I will drop kick you across this room, then out of the building from the highest window." Her voice was low and Cain knew she meant every word.

"She'll be watched at all times," Payton said. "I have a...she's involved with a buddy of mine. A good friend who served as a Navy Seal. He's the best at what he does and he'll keep her from harm."

"The guy in her bedroom," Cain asked. "If you pimped out my sister to make this happen, so help me Christ, whatever Alyssa has planned for you is nothing compared to what I'll do to your sorry ass."

Payton backed away with his hands up. Cain had a moment to remember he was armed, but kept moving. It wasn't until Drew stepped between them that he stopped. He glared at the men, but didn't back down.

"She and Mr. Cunningham hooked up on their own. I swear. Michael called Payton a few days ago to ask him about her and that was before we found out where the money was going. He was asking if she was attached and to tell Payton that he was seeing her. He didn't know; none of us did."

"Michael Cunningham of Cunningham and Cunningham? I know him. Well, my father knew him. He is some big deal buyer in New York. He buys and sells...well, everything, I guess. Last I heard he was making arrangements to purchase fallen rail cars as they come up on shore. He nearly had that in the bag, last I heard." Alyssa sat at her desk and began clicking on the computer. "Here, look Cain. He's the real deal and almost as rich as we are."

Cain walked around the desk, but still wasn't convinced that Payton hadn't set this up. He liked the guy and he was really good to his sister, but that didn't mean he wouldn't kill him if he got Grace hurt. Cain sat in the chair that his wife got up from and started skimming the articles about the man who his sister was seeing.

"It says here he has a son. What happened to his wife?" Cain looked up when no one answered. "Drew? I asked you a question."

"He never married. Terrance Michael Cunningham is the result of a long affair Michael had with a woman he never really liked." Payton sat down, took the file, and slid a picture across to them. "She was killed about a year and a half after the kid was born. So far as we can tell, she never had a thing to do with either of them after he was born."

Cain read over the file again. There was something he was missing, he knew it, but he couldn't quite put his finger on it. He looked up when Payton cleared his throat. From the look on his face, he knew that whatever it was, he wasn't going to like it.

"Your sister is in deep shit. Grace has been harassed for several months, it seems. Michael said that the calls and the threats have become quite violent. He said that whoever is threatening her has also targeted him and his son." Payton shifted in his seat. "Has she ever said anything to you about it? Not even a slip of the tongue?"

"No," Cain said sadly. "She talks with Jazzie the most, but I'm sure she would have told me if she'd said anything. Gracie moved to New York and, as you know, doesn't come home all that much. She left, literally, in the middle of the night while I was away at school." He pulled Alyssa into his lap when she came to him. "How bad is it, Payton? Is it as bad as the rest?"

Payton pulled out another bunch of papers. "Michael took the tape from her machine, had a copy made, and sent it to me. She doesn't know and will probably be pissed at him when she finds out, so let's keep this between us. He claims she's not heard the messages. She told him that she doesn't listen to them, simply erases them as soon as she thinks about it."

"But you don't believe her, do you?"

Payton shook his head.

"What does this Cunningham person know? Has she shared anything with him?"

"He told me yesterday that he was taking her to his house and sitting her down and talking to her. Whether or not that happened, I don't know. Michael said that he would come with her this weekend even if she didn't invite him. He…he's in love with her."

Cain hugged Alyssa tighter. He had to ask, but he wasn't sure he could without breaking down. He looked at Drew then at Payton. He took a deep breath. "My mother, she's been trying to kill us all since the beginning, right?"

Payton nodded.

"Why, do we know?"

He shook his head this time.

"Then how do you know it's her? I mean, maybe she's taking the money because, hell, I don't know, maybe she thinks she's owed it…Holy Christ, my father. She's taking this because of my father. And we're all…"

"We're all paying because she feels we are the cause of his death," Alyssa finished for him. "What are we going to do to finish this? Because I, for one, want this over with."

~~~

Guinevere watched the house. Well, she watched the gate. She had been told by Ginny that if anyone got by her without her warning someone, she'd be hurting. Guinevere huffed. Ginny was becoming entirely too full of herself. Closing her eyes against the small pain that was just behind her ears, Guinevere thought about the past few weeks.

Ginny was the least of their problems. Verrie was becoming impossible to control. Her violent outrages were getting to be messy. Just last night it had taken her over three hours to clean up the blood and gore after one of her episodes. And the man…Guinevere felt her stomach lurch at what she'd done to him.

Not only had she eviscerated him, but she'd cut off his cock and every other appendage that he had. His fingers were put into his mouth, along with his cock. But it was what she'd done with his entrails that made her think of going to the bushes and throwing up again. He'd been decorated with them. And if that wasn't enough, she'd even draped them around the headboard and foot board like a canopy in a little girl's room. Guinevere hadn't even known there was that much belly in a person.

"You loved it and you know it. You're just jealous that I can make murder a work of art." Guinevere stiffened when Verrie's voice entered her head. "And don't be such a prude. You've killed your fair share of men over the past few years. Like those idiots you hired to take out the money-grubbing whore."

"Killing for hire and killing for pleasure are two different things altogether. I killed those 'idiots,' as you called them, because they fucked up. You killed that man because...why did you kill him?" Guinevere watched a car pull into the drive, but not go through the gates before it pulled away. It didn't enter, but simply pulled in. She didn't bother making note of the license plate number.

"Because I could. And it sounded like fun. Have you ever stuck a knife into someone's soft parts and felt the way it slid in? It's quite invigorating, let me tell you. Then there is the way the guts smell when you unearth them." Verrie made a noise that reminded Guinevere of kissing and her stomach lurched again. "You need to have a little more fun. Think of the possibilities."

Guinevere did and she ran for the bushes behind her and threw up. And when there was nothing else she heaved some more. By the time she'd gotten back to her post and settled, she noticed that the gates were coming to a quiet close.

"Well fuck." She looked up and down the street and didn't see anything moving. She didn't know if someone had come onto the grounds or off of them. She was in so much trouble that she was nearly sick again. Thinking hard, she tried to decide what she should do. If she didn't report it then no one would be the wiser. If there was someone else on the property, which she reasoned had to be what had happened, then she was clear. She'd been told to tell if someone left, not entered. She sat back down on the grassy area and tried to calm herself. If she was stressed or too upset then one of the others would come back.

She must have dosed, or one of the others came by to check on her, because the next thing she knew she was back at the house they rented. The smell nearly made her sick again. Guinevere sat up on the couch and noticed that her entire front was covered in blood. Her nose had bled again. It was happening more and more and that frightened her a great deal. She went to the bathroom to clean up and found that someone had made a bloody mess in there.

Thankfully there was no body this time, just a lot of blood. It took her twenty minutes to clean it up. Then she stepped into the shower and cleaned herself and her clothes. They didn't have a washer and she couldn't take these bloody things to the laundromat.

When she stepped out of the shower and glanced into the mirror Guinevere froze. She'd not seen her for a very long time. Guinnie was staring at her for a long time and, when she spoke, Guinevere had a premonition that scared her more than Verrie ever did.

"We're all going to die very soon by Gracie's hand. And when we do, I will be at peace for the first time in all my life."

Chapter 13

Michael watched Grace. She would sit for a few minutes then get up to pace. He was glad they'd taken his plane instead of flying commercial; she would never have been able to stand the flight otherwise. He glanced over at Trace and his dog playing on the floor. And Trace would have had to leave the dog behind, which he was sure wouldn't have been easy for either of them.

"I don't know why you have to come along. I can very well go to a family dinner by myself. Believe it or not, I've been taking care of myself long before you came along." She paced some more before she continued. "And as for where you're sleeping, it will not be in my bed. Cain will have a fit and I, for once, agree with him."

He had learned last night that there was no reasoning with her when she was on a roll. If he just let her run down then he could convince her his way was the best and she'd go along. Well, that had worked in theory. He smiled when he thought about the trip to the airport and her thinking all the way there they were simply dropping her off and not going with her.

"Grace, don't you want us to come and meet your family?" Trace said from his position on the floor. "I can't wait to meet them all. Especially Sin. She sounds like she is so cool. Do you think she'll let me shoot her gun?"

When both Grace and Michael answered "no" at the same time Trace rolled on the floor laughing. He'd gotten them both and

Michael laughed when Grace got down on the floor and started tickling him. He thought his son was the smartest person he knew. Still laughing, he pulled out his cell phone when it rang.

"I have a car waiting to pick you up at the airport. Someone will meet you in the terminal," Payton told him as soon as he answered. "Did you have any problems convincing her that you should come with her?"

"I didn't tell her until we got there. It seemed the best way to go under the circumstances. She's a little ticked off at me right now." Payton laughed as Michael continued. "She's going on about where I'm sleeping. I think I might stay in a hotel just to piss her off." He heard her snort and knew that she was listening to him. "Then again, I might want to find myself someone else to have a good time with, one that isn't such a prude."

"You're playing with fire, my man. Sin, my wife, and you will have a lot in common. You both can scare the shit out of a grown man from fifty paces. Don't fuck with one or you fuck with them all. Learned that the hard way," Payton said with a laugh. "And Alyssa. Damn, that girl can peel the hide off a man with just her voice. She's fucking scary."

"I knew her father. Now there was a scary man. He could have you convinced that whatever he wanted had been your idea all along and you'd not know he'd taken you until you were sitting in your car. I loved doing business with the man." Michael laughed at the memory. "I'm hoping the daughter is much like the man. If she is, then she'll be a worthy adversary."

"You've no idea. That woman can turn a dime into a million with just her smile. And a fundraiser? She's brutal. Last month during a board meeting she challenged each one of her department heads to a basketball game. The winner, if you want to call it that, got a month off with pay. The fine print got the guy. His month off was him working in the shelter and, at the end of his month, she gave him a fat bonus for being such a good sport about it." Payton snorted as he continued. "Damned if the man didn't think that the whole challenge had been his idea."

Michael was looking forward to meeting them all. Especially Cain. Cain had kept his family together for his entire life and still did when necessary. Plus, he wanted to make sure there were no hard feelings about him being in Grace's bedroom the last time he'd called. Not that he was going to deny why he was there, but he did want the man to know that his intentions were honorable. Michael heard the pilot say they were about twenty minutes from the airport. He told Payton.

"A man by the name of Winston will be picking you up. I just sent a picture to your phone so you'll know what he looks like. We'll talk more when you get here. Oh, there's a dinner thing tonight. A sort of meet and greet for you and the kid." Michael heard Payton talking to someone else. "Sin said to tell you that she's booked you time at the gun range for Sunday. I think she wants to see if you're all that."

Michael grinned. If the truth be known, this sister scared him the least of all. She was military like him and she'd be someone who would either have your back or have a knife at your throat. He grinned at the description that Grace had given about her.

"She's a twin and the exact polar opposite of Lilly Pad. Where one is a school teacher who wouldn't say shit if her life depended on it, the other would make a sailor blush and probably has. Sin is a bit...abrasive, but she's loyal. If I had to go into a bar, she'd be the one on the tables dancing and singing at the top of her lungs, but the first one to throw the punch if she felt a brawl was going to be fun. I love them all and wouldn't trade them for the world."

"And you miss them," he said to her. She burst into tears and nodded. He'd held her until she fell asleep then crawled into the bed with her.

Michael laughed at the thought of being tested by someone. "Tell her I am. I'll see you soon."

~~~

The ride to the house was quiet. Trace was nervous; Grace could tell. She was too. What if they wanted to know everything? She glanced over at Michael as he talked on his cell phone. What if

103

they wanted to know what he was doing here? She didn't even know herself.

Of course, she knew they were aware of them coming. She'd called Jazzie when the plane had taken off to let her know to find a place for Trace and Michael to stay. She'd told her that Payton had already made arrangements for them to stay at their house. She wasn't sure who the "they" were and was afraid to ask. She put her hand on her belly again to try and settle it.

"There's probably some ginger ale in the cooler if you want it."

She looked over at Michael when he spoke.

"For your belly. Ginger ale usually does the trick with Trace when he's got a nervous belly."

"I'm not nervous," she snapped. "I'm wondering what Cain will think about you barging in on his household. He's not a very nice man when he's pissed." She looked at him when he threw back his head and laughed. Her entire body felt it. She wanted to snuggle up into his chest and stay there. Grace looked away when she felt the tears threaten. He was going to get hurt, maybe even killed, and there was nothing she could do about it.

"Come here, love. I want to hold you."

She thought about telling him no, but he pulled her to him anyway.

"I want to tell you something. Something that you should know before your family asks."

When he didn't say anything more she sat up and looked at him. "What? I'm supposing you've been talking to them all along without my knowledge, right?"

He nodded.

"Well, what could you possibly tell me now that they don't already know?"

He reached into his jacket pocket and handed her a small box. She looked at it for several seconds before she looked back up at him. The little blue box was something she'd never expected.

"Open it, Grace," he told her softly.

She shook her head.

"Open the box and tell me yes so that I can slip it onto your lovely finger."

She started to reach out and touch it. Her fingers were trembling and her heart was pounding hard. She closed her hand before she could touch it and looked up at him. "What if…what if you decide that you don't want me after you meet my family? Shouldn't you wait until after?" After what, she wasn't sure, but he was already opening the box and taking out the ring. "Oh, Michael, it's beautiful."

It was a beautiful square cut yellow diamond surrounded by small, oval-shaped sapphires and rubies. The setting was on a wide band that had vines that looked to be spun gold that encircled the band and held the stones in place. She fell in love with it the moment she saw it. She was shaking when he slipped it just over her first knuckle.

"I don't need to know the 'what ifs,' love. You've had my heart since the moment you pulled me to your mouth with my tie. I've never wanted a woman like I did you at that moment, and had there not been a room full of people, I would have taken you right there." He slipped it past the second knuckle. "Then I got to know you, the real Grace Anne Waite, and there was nothing I wanted more than to spend the rest of my life with you. Please say yes so that I can kiss you properly."

She leaned down to him to do just that when she suddenly pulled back. His moan nearly had her smile. "What about Trace? He has to have a say in this—"

"Will you just kiss him already?" Trace said from behind her. "I can't keep holding my hand over my eyes forever. I want you as my mom, okay? Sheesh, you people can't do anything without a million questions."

She started crying the moment her mouth touched Michael's. "I love you," she said. "I love you both so very much."

Everyone was waiting on the front porch of Cain's house when they pulled up. She didn't wait for the car to come to a complete stop before she was out and rushing to her family. She was crying so hard that it took her several runs through them all before she realized that her mother wasn't there. When she started to ask, Alyssa shook her head and pulled them all inside. She introduced Michael and Trace to her family.

"Holy shit, look at that rock," Alyssa said as soon as she noticed the ring. "Oh my, I didn't know you two had gotten that far just yet."

"He just asked her," Trace said to the group. "It took her forever to answer him, then he had to kiss her." He made a noise much like a choking victim. "And all they do is kiss anyway. I can't wait until it wears off or something."

Cain kneeled down to Trace. "It never wears off, I'm happy to say. And who would this little fellow be?" Cain didn't touch the puppy until Trace offered it to him. And, once he did, Cain took the little guy into his hands gently. Grace knew her brother liked animals, and especially dogs.

"Grace helped me name him. They were going to throw him out into the street but she helped me take him to the vet. We had to give him a name that he'd have to live up to. So we called him Walter Stuffinpuppy the Fourth." Trace looked at Grace then back at Cain. "She said you have a little boy who would like to pet him. But she said I had to be real careful of them both on account of them both being babies."

Cain looked up at her. "That's right. His name is Connor. He's almost three. But he doesn't like to be called a baby anymore. He has a temper like your Grace does. So why don't you come with me and I'll introduce you." Cain took Trace with him and he didn't look back once.

"Come on in. We have a great deal to talk about and even more to share," Alyssa said as she hugged her again. "I'm so glad you could make it. I've wanted to have you here for so long."

"I wasn't really given a choice. I was taken to the airport and then rushed into his plane before I had a chance to decide." She smiled at her sister-in-law. "And I was just home for Lilly Pad's wedding three months ago."

"Yes, but now you're going to be here for a little while longer." She stopped at Alyssa's words. "You did know you were staying until this is over, right? They told you that you're being stalked and couldn't go back to your building?"

"No, they did not. And I'm sure they have a wonderful reason for not telling me, too." Grace went to the office with Alyssa. "I can't stay very long. I've a business to run until…well, until. I have employees to take…son of a bitch."

"Now, Grace…I don't know what you're thinking of doing, but please don't do it in the house. I just had all the carpets cleaned and I so don't want to have to explain to the housekeeper again why there is blood on the walls. It's too hard to get out of damask." Alyssa sat down and patted the seat next to her. "Come on. We'll plan their demise together. Let me tell you what I know."

After Alyssa told her that Michael had made arrangements to have her business moved to his building and had given her employees a month off with pay she was seeing red. Then she told her about the catalogue. That made her so pissed that her head hurt from it.

"I assumed, like everyone else, that you knew about the cover. You were in it so I guess…he didn't tell you that he approved of the cover? That person who took the picture said you'd sell more undergarments from that one picture than any other thing in it." Alyssa pulled up the advanced copy of the catalogue she'd been sent as a frequent buyer. "I have to tell you that I've never seen you look so decadent before. In fact, I wasn't even sure it was you until Cain said so."

"I'm going to kill him and whoever else was in on this. No, wait, murder is too good. I'm going to chop his dick up into little pieces and serve it to him for his dinner. Of all the underhanded, sneaky things…what the hell were they thinking?"

"I was thinking I wanted you to be safe and with me. I was thinking that if I could make one thing easier for you then I'd do it. But mostly, I was thinking I'd make you happy because I love you."

She turned to see Michael as he stood in the doorway.

"Alyssa, could you please give us some privacy? I think that Grace wants to tell me how much she appreciates me."

Alyssa laughed, but left the room. Michael reached over and clicked the lock as soon as the door closed behind her. She knew she was in trouble the moment he turned back to her. She didn't know this look like she'd been able to figure out the others. This one was…well, hot.

"You shouldn't do things without telling me. I like to run my own businesses. How would you like it if I came into your office and started spouting off orders and changing things?" She started to back away as he advanced. "You have no right to be mad at me when you are the one doing things that I didn't know about."

"I'm not mad. And whenever you want to come to my office and learn the business I'll be more than happy to show you around. And as for spouting off orders, you're welcome to that too. I hate to have to be the heavy, and having someone run the daily crap is fine with me." He took off his jacket and tossed it over a chair, a sign that he was going to strip her down as well. "Grace, come here. It will go so much better for you if you don't make me have to chase you."

She was suddenly nervous. "You…what do you think you're going to do to me? You can't mean to have sex with me in my brother's house. He'll have…stop right there."

He did stop, but as he did he pulled his belt off. For some reason the sight of him pulling the leather through the loops on his pants made her pussy tighten and soak her panties. He tossed it toward the chair. When he started to unbutton his sleeves and roll them up she had to swallow several times before she could think about speaking.

"Come here," he said softly. "I promise you that my spanking you will hurt less if you let me do it my way."

She looked up at his face to see if he was serious. He apparently was.

"If you think I'm going to let you paddle my ass, you're nuttier than a fruitcake. I'm a grown woman, not some little kid who needs to be disciplined." But when he reached for her she didn't fight him. "Michael, please…"

108

His mouth took hers. There was just no other way to describe it. His tongue plunged into her mouth and parlayed with her own. His hands were everywhere, touching and pulling, taking her clothing off and baring her to him. Before she knew it she was standing before him in just her panties.

He pulled her with him to the chair. She was on fire for him and, at this point, couldn't have denied him anything. When she was across his lap, her ass across his groin, she could feel his cock. She moaned when he cupped her ass.

"I don't know whether I want to fuck you over that desk or pink up your ass then fuck you. Christ, you can make me harder than I've ever been." He rubbed his hand over her ass cheek and she moaned.

When his hand connected hard with her bottom, she moaned. She could come. Right now, she could very easily come this way. He seemed to realize that because the third and the forth blows were harder, but it didn't matter. She was beyond anything but him. Before his hand took her over the edge she found herself standing and leaning over the chair. Panting hard, she felt him behind her and turned her head at her shoulder to watch him free his cock.

"You're going to pay for this, Grace. I'm not sure how much pleasure I can give you right now so if you find release, Christ, you'd better take it." He plunged deep. His cock seemed to touch her throat. "Fuck, you're so tight. And wet. I'm not going to...fuck."

He came hard. Even as his cock filled her and his hands held her to him, she followed him. Reaching between her legs, she found her slick clit and pinched it. Her second then third climax was shuddering through her when he joined her fingers between her legs and brought her again. Grace felt the world fade away as she slipped into semi-consciousness.

Chapter 14

Thomas pushed the buzzer again. It seemed like forever before someone answered. He hated being put off and was sure that was what Michael was doing. First he'd gotten by him at work and now he was avoiding him at his house. The cocksucker was going to answer his question or hell would be paid.

"Where's my stepbrother? I want to talk to him right fucking now. And I don't want to hear any shit about him being unavailable. He, fucking, is always available." Thomas took a deep breath and tried to reign in his temper. "He said he'd meet with me today and he's late."

"Mr. Cunningham is not in residence, sir. If you would like to leave your name, then perhaps if he calls in as he usually does, I will give him—"

"I just told you who I was. I'm Thomas Rutherford Cunningham, his fucking stepbrother. Don't you fucking people listen? And what do you mean 'not in residence?' What the fuck does that mean?" Thomas looked over at the girl in his car. Actually, he'd been surprised to see her there. He neither knew her name nor where she'd come from. He wondered if she'd been someone he'd picked up or someone that had just decided to hop in his car. He had no clue. She was giving him the thumbs up, whatever that meant.

"It means that he is not at home. And I would prefer that you toned down your language a bit, sir. There is absolutely no reason for so much profanity."

Thomas felt his head tighten. Yeah, he was high and a little drunk, but he knew that, as a Cunningham, servants did not talk to their betters the way this asshole was. His mother let them talk to her that way and so did his father but, by God, they were not going to speak to him like that. He started to tell the little prick that when his cell phone went off.

He barked his name into it and closed his eyes. There was that white light of pain again, the one that told him he either needed to take it down a notch or go into rehab for a few weeks. He decided that he'd like neither one, but taking it down was much better than no drugs. No fucking way.

"We didn't have a meeting. I told you I'd get back to you and that's what I had planned to do," Michael said in that calm voice of his. "What the fuck are you doing threatening my staff?"

Thomas tried to remember threatening the man on the other end of the intercom, but couldn't seem to make his head work. Before he could say that he'd not done it, that the servants were not to be trusted, Michael gave him a clue.

"Matt said if you ever talk to his wife that way again he will castrate you, then feed your tiny dick to the birds. What the hell is wrong with you threatening a woman in the first place?"

Michael took a deep breath, but before he continued Thomas broke in. He just wanted them all to do what they said they'd do so he could get this fucking business over with. "She wouldn't tell me where you were. I've been calling your office all morning and you didn't answer. Then I tried your home. You aren't there either. The fucking servant said you weren't 'in-residence,' whatever the fuck that means."

Thomas looked at the girl again. She was laughing and he knew it was at him. He'd take care of her right fucking now. Slipping open the car door, he didn't even close it before he doubled his fist up and hit her right in the face. She fell back against the window with a nice pop and he tried to concentrate on his stepbrother.

112

"…when I get back. I'm not going to make a decision until then." There was a slight pause and Thomas wondered what he'd missed. "Are you listening to me? I want you to stay away from my house and my servants. In fact, I want you to stay the hell away from anything that belongs to me. You got it?"

"Yeah, I got it. But the girl…what's her name? Wadders…Waite, she's not around either. Where is she? With you, I suppose?" Thomas was going to get the girl, Grace, if it was the last thing he'd do. "You give me her phone number and I'll pretend none of this ever—"

"You stay the hell away from my future wife, do you hear me, Thomas?" Michael said with a tone that he'd only ever heard once before, and he'd been afraid then too. "If you so much as go near her, I will hunt you down and kill you slowly. The same for my son. You don't want to test me—"

"I didn't touch the little shit. I don't care what he said happened. I was following him out of the building and he disappeared. I thought he went in that building on Ninth, the one you've been whining about, but I couldn't get in to get him." The silence at the other end made him think Michael had hung up on him. When Michael started speaking this time, Thomas knew he'd pushed him too far.

"You aren't to come near anything I own ever again. And if I hear of you doing anything, including breathing the same airspace as my family, there won't be a hole you can hide deep enough in, nor will there be a place that I won't find you. You will pray for death before I'm through with you. Do I make myself perfectly clear?"

Thomas was terrified. He knew what his stepbrother had been in the Special Forces. He knew what he'd been doing the entire time he'd been in. He'd heard the stories or the half stories that Michael and his father talked about. And he'd even cared enough to look it up. Michael was a hired killer. And not only that, but he was fucking good at it.

"I hear you." His voice was not nearly a brave as he'd wanted and it squeaked a bit and that pissed him off. "But if I catch them out, all bets are off." He closed the phone and leaned his head back against the seat. The small mewling sound made him remember the girl next to him. He looked over at her without lifting his head. Just what he fucking needed.

The window was covered in blood. And her face was fat and also bloodied. He knew he'd hit her, but he also knew he'd not hit her that hard. He hated whiny people, especially whiny whores. Shifting in the seat to get a better look at her, he realized he didn't have a clue who she was and he honestly didn't care. She turned to look at him with her one good eye and started to speak.

"Shut up," he snarled at her. "You just shut the fuck up. And if you think you're going to get to a hospital anytime soon, then you're fucking out of luck. I just gotta figure out what to do with you." He tried to think, but her crying and whining again had him reach over and wrap his hands around her throat. He let her go when she shut up.

She was dead. As soon as he realized he'd killed her, he laughed. "Now, brother dearest, you're so fucked. What will your little family think when they find a dead hooker on your doorstep?"

Thomas got out of his car and walked to the other side. He was pulling her out of the passenger's side door when he thought of something really funny. If whatshername... Grace found out about her future husband's former life and this hooker on the lawn she would come running to him in no time. Yes, Thomas thought as he kicked the hooker again, things were about to get really good for him.

Thomas went back to his house after making a quick trip to his buddy's. After scoring a few grams of some sweet stuff and hitting it with him Thomas was feeling pretty good. So good, in fact, that he didn't care that his phone was ringing or that he was driving a little on the fast side. When he finally pulled into his drive he simply left the car running and went inside. Life was good.

The pounding on the door had him sitting up in bed. He didn't know what time it was, but he was sure he'd only just lain down. He was nearly to the door when he saw the flashing lights. Stopping in the living room he tried to remember if he'd done anything wrong to

114

warrant the police showing up at his house. Thinking hard, he started to go back to the bedroom and escape. He needed to leave, and right fucking now. Picking up his gun out of the dresser near his window Thomas opened the window and slipped out. He was nearly to the back of the lot when he saw the cop.

Fucking no way was he going in. He wasn't sure who was more surprised by the gun in his hand going off, him or the cop, but the guy just sort of crumpled to the ground, his head suddenly a mess. Thomas had a few moments of pure glee that he'd gotten the drop on the guy when he realized he'd just killed a cop. Before he knew it he was running for his life and there were fucking cops everywhere.

Mother fuck.

~~~

Verrie watched the news lead story run again. The stupid cock sucker had killed a fucking cop. Not to mention the debutante that he'd killed earlier. What the hell he'd been thinking killing a girl on camera was…it didn't bear thinking. She started to turn off the television when they showed the scene again. She smiled. He'd done a very good job of killing the girl; she was impressed. Not that they showed much. Some blurred pictures of the girl on the ground and the frantic interview with the butler at the home of Cunningham. Verrie wondered, not for the first time, if all men simply had a brain in their dicks and, every time they came, a little more of it leaked out. She swore that that was why there were so many old men in nursing homes. They'd fucked themselves stupid.

There was an all-points bulletin out for Thomas Cunningham. The FBI said that they were taking precautions. She couldn't figure out what the hell they were doing in on it when the family of the dead bitch came on. The senator of New York. Well, when Thomas did something up, he certainly didn't do it in half measures.

Killing a senator's daughter was big news. And even bigger news was that she had only been seventeen when she'd been murdered. Verrie turned off the television and sat on the dirty couch. They were running out of time. The money had arrived yesterday, but Ginny had insisted that they try very hard not to spend it like they had done with what they'd brought with them. Verrie snorted. Like she gave a good fuck what she said. Reaching between the cushions she pulled out the stash that she knew Guinevere had stuffed there yesterday. Twenty grand would go a long way to having a good time. Smiling, she started for the door only to stop when Ginny started in on her.

"No," she snapped. "I told you we have to lay low. And if you kill anyone right now, especially right now, we're never going to see this thing to the end."

"Like you care. All you want to do is fuck that boy, Cain. Well, he ain't gonna have you. In case it escaped your notice, you are his mother as far as he's concerned." Verrie felt the pain from the other woman. "And on top of that, you're old. Nobody that looks like him is gonna wanna fuck someone as old as you are."

The pain in Verrie's head was immense. But she didn't move or so much as acknowledge it. She stood still while the blood trickled from her nose and ears.

"I fucking hate you. You've been a fucking pain in our ass since the first time you showed up. Why? Why do you have to be so cruel?"

Verrie started to answer, but she couldn't speak until Ginny let her.

"I'm going to destroy you when this is over. I'm going to make sure that you are never allowed to come out ever again."

"Fucking try it, cunt, and see where it gets you. You may be the top dog now, but I'm the one that pulled the strings. If I want I'll murder myself a cop and get us put into jail for the rest of our lives. And you know who will have to be the first when we get there. Your little pansy ass would never survive past the first night." They had been in jail twice now and, both times, Verrie had been the one who'd kept them together. "I might just let you be the first and then see how much you need me just for the fun of it."

Ginny went away and left her to herself. Verrie sat on the couch and thought about how they had become. She knew there was probably a technical term for what they had developed into, but she

116

neither cared enough to look it up, nor did she give a good shit. They just had become.

Verrie knew that she couldn't make any one of them not appear again. And none of them knew who was in charge, but all of them knew that it wasn't Guinevere. She knew that Ginny and the others couldn't survive. And if they didn't, or worse yet, got caught and put into a hospital, she might as well be dead. They would keep them so doped up all the time there would be no way for any of them to be very productive.

Being first, as in the host, was Guinevere's role. Ginny had come to Guinevere when things had been too hard for her. Ginny the child had a horrific childhood. Over the first years of her life, the most fragile ones, her father and mother had abused Guinevere to no end. Locking her in closest, starving her, or worse, making her eat well beyond what she wanted were just a few of the things they'd done to the already unstable child. Then when things had gotten bad, or out of her control, Guinevere would become the docile, sometimes self-abusing Ginny again. It wasn't until later, in her preteen years, that she'd turned to her.

Verrie had been the bad-assed Guinevere. Guinevere would turn to her when things got to be overwhelming. And Verrie would take care of it. The boy who had made fun of where she'd lived had been in a diving accident. A little bit of drugs from Guinevere's mother's array of barbiturates in his water bottle made him dizzy and he slipped off the high dive during practice and hit his head. He'd died almost instantly.

Then there was the little girl from the library that had made fun of Guinevere's clothes. They weren't new, nor were they very clean. That little girl was mauled to death by a dog. Verrie had known the dog was wild and had let it smell the girl's shirt every day for two weeks while Verrie beat him. When he'd been allowed out of his pen and found himself with his supposed tormentor, he'd gone wild. The girl never had a chance and had died from massive injuries. Verrie felt bad for his death. She hated to see animals killed.

Over the years, she'd gotten better at hiding the murders. Then one day, she simply didn't care. She killed her first man at the house

Guinevere and Roscoe had shared. It had been a dump and he was in jail on some crime that he'd always told them that he'd been framed for. As far as Verrie had always thought, Roscoe was an idiot. But the man she'd brought home because she'd been lonely and horny had proved to be so much fun that she'd made a habit of killing men whenever she could.

They'd been having sex. Of course, that was another thing. Verrie simply loved sex. But this guy with his huge cock had satisfied her completely. She asked him if she could tie him up. He'd told her that he wasn't really into that sort of shit, but he'd tie her up. She really wanted to bond him to the bed and he wasn't playing fair so she pulled the gun and cuffed him to the bed.

She thought maybe he was excited. His cock was still semi-hard and she'd been happy to see that he hadn't screamed at her. Guinevere's kids were just down the hall and she didn't want them to barge into her fun. When she'd sat over him and told him what she had planned, he looked like he thought she was insane. The pillow over his face probably gave him the first indication that she was serious.

Every time his cock became flaccid she'd suck him off. No man could resist her mouth and she made him hard almost immediately. Well, she could at first. After the fourth time she'd cut him he was harder to…well, get hard. She smiled at her pun. By the time he'd lost consciousness the first time she'd already cut him enough that she knew he was going to have to die. Then, when she'd gagged him, the real fun had begun.

At first Verrie had experimented, played with the way she cut him. She was inexperienced in the way she killed him; she could see that now. But as the years had gone by her work with a blade had become precise and perfect until she knew when she had a man in her clutches he was hers until she'd had enough. Killing a man slowly, she could bleed them out and still have her fun. She was able to make the killing last for days now rather than the few hours she'd had the first time. She thought of the people she had killed that night and decided to go to the furnace room and check on her latest victims.

She'd had to hide them quickly before one of the others came to her. Verrie hadn't expected anyone to come by and nearly catch her in the act of having fun with the man she'd picked up at the bar the night before. She wasn't stupid. She was a murderer, but not that. No, never that. She'd wrapped him in the throw on the back of the disgusting couch and hidden him behind it when someone had started ringing the door bell.

Her landlord at the door simply wouldn't leave. Finally, after an hour of him asking about the different aspects of the apartment, she'd taken one of Ginny's pots and hit him over the head with it. It took her forever to get the landlord's body down to the furnace room and even longer to get the first man she'd killed down there too. She'd had to hide the fucking prick who'd wanted to make sure the stove was working correctly before he came up missing. Now she had the landlord all wrapped up in plastic and the dead man from earlier both tucked in the basement. She needed to find somewhere to put them, and fast.

She made her way to the basement and was trying to decide the best way to move over four hundred pounds of bloody dead weight then the fucking debutante killer popped out from behind the furnace.

"You have to help me. I can't go…the police were at my house and now I can't go back."

She stared at him as he continued to rant.

"They think I killed somebody. I didn't…I don't think I did. My stepbrother and that cunt, they framed me."

"They have you on tape, you fucking moron. There was a security camera at the gate where you left her body. When you kill someone, you can't leave any witnesses." She smiled at him, thinking that was a good plan. "You get in touch with your brother yet?"

"He's not my brother," he snarled at her. "He's my fucking stepbrother."

When he lunged at her, Verrie smiled bigger and pulled the trigger on her gun.

Chapter 15

Michael had to go home. He didn't want to. He wanted to stay here in Ohio and get to know Grace's family and enjoy them. But the problem with his brother and his mother's hysterics was too much for his dad to handle alone. He was tossing stuff into his case when Trace came into the room. Without stopping, he glanced at him and grimaced. Trace was upset.

"We'll only be gone long enough to get this fixed then come right back. Grace said she'd even watch Walter for you and make sure he was—"

"I don't want to go. I want to...I'm afraid to go back with you."

Michael turned to look at his son as he continued.

"If I go back, Thomas will find me and hurt me. He's told me that before. And maybe..."

Michael was almost afraid to ask. "Maybe what, son? What else makes you not want to go back with me? I promise you that Thomas won't come near you. He'll not get past me, I swear."

Trace sat in the chair near the bed and looked at his shoes. Michael knew his son well enough to know that he needed to process. He was a brilliant little boy, but he was more of a thinker than he was a fly by the seat of his ass sort of kid. He waited also, knowing that rushing him would only upset him to the point where he'd clam up all together.

"Grace will leave us." Trace looked at him now. "She'll think she'll be doing us this great big favor, but she won't. My heart will hurt if she isn't here when we get back. If I stay..." he said as he got up to pace. "If I stay, then I can make sure she's doesn't leave us. She wouldn't leave me if I'm here. I can...I'll make sure to call you if anything happens too."

Michael had been afraid of the same thing. He'd even gone so far as to ask Cain and the others to watch her to make sure that she didn't leave. He loved her with all his heart and he was sure she loved them both too, but she would bolt at the first opportunity.

"Your grandmother will be disappointed. She's hoping that you'll help her not think about what Thomas has done and give her hugs." It was a cheap trick he knew, but the thought of leaving Trace where he couldn't watch him was scary. "I can't watch you if you're not with me."

"I sort of already called Grandma. I told her that Grace loves us, but... I told her I didn't want to lose her. I need her too much to not want to be with her." Michael couldn't help but be very proud of his son. "She told me that if you were okay with me staying here to protect the woman I love then she was going to be fine with it too."

Trace flushed and Michael knew there was more. "What did she make you give her back? I know there was something. Mom doesn't just let an opportunity like this pass her by without extracting some sort of payment. Dishes for a month? Or was it something like weeding her flower beds for the summer?"

"She said I had to hug her at the mall," Trace said with venom in his voice. "I don't like hugs. Why would she make me do something like that when she knows it's going to embarrass me to death? What if one of my friends sees me doing it? I'll never live it down, Dad."

Michael laughed. It was the first really good laugh he'd had all day.

"Because she knows it will embarrass you. When you do it, make sure you try to pull it off like it's no big deal. She won't do that again." Standing, he knelt before Trace and looked up at him. This was as serious as it got. "Thomas is accused of murder; I know

122

you know that. But do you know what else he's done?" Trace shook his head. "He's also accused of murdering two men and hiding them in the basement of an apartment complex. The police might not have known he'd done it if somebody hadn't called them. It's going to get ugly, son, and people are going to talk about this for a long time. Thomas killed four people, four innocent people."

"Did he do it? I know what the news lady is saying, but do you think he did it?"

Michael wasn't positive, but he didn't want to say it out loud yet. He didn't want to admit just yet that he thought for sure Thomas had done it. He didn't answer Trace, but stood to finish packing. "Stay with Grace. I know I don't have to tell you that, but for my peace of mind, please don't leave her side. The others, all of her family, is going to help you watch her, but she's tricky." Michael smiled when Trace snorted. "She is and you know it. Thomas is in the hospital right now, but there are others...other people trying to hurt her and they might try to get to her by hurting you. Don't let them. All right?"

"Yeah. Aunt Sin said that she was going to give me a whistle. That I was to blow it in the sucker's ear if someone tried to grab me. She's sort of scary, huh?"

That was an understatement, Michael thought. The woman was nursing a bullet wound that she'd gotten a few months ago during a raid on a house which was harboring a known cell that was plotting against the United States. She'd been shot because she went in first and came out last. She'd been hurt because she was the bravest woman he'd ever met.

"Yes. But she knows her stuff. So does her husband Payton and Lilliane's husband Shamus. If they tell you to do something, I want you to listen to them as if I were telling you. They'll keep you safe. Grace too."

Trace came to sit on the bed and he played with one of the few things Michael was taking back with him. He waited for Trace to say whatever it was he needed. He was shocked when he finally spoke.

"I have a friend, Taylor Bennett. His dad just got married last year. His new mom was okay, he said, and he was excited about having someone to have fun with." Trace didn't look up as he spoke, his voice low and tense. "Then about a month ago, she decided that she wanted her own kid and had his dad put him in a different school. Taylor has to stay there all the time and wear this uniform like he's in the army or something. He only gets to come home once in a while. I miss him."

"I wouldn't do that to you," Grace said from the doorway. "Never in a million years would I send you away from your father, and especially not away from me."

"But what if you get tired of me? I'm not your kid, you know. I'm his." Trace pointed at him, and Michael nearly told him to take it down a notch as his voice had hardened. "And my mom and dad weren't even married when I was born. She didn't want me."

Grace walked into the room and sat in the chair. Michael knew that this was something the two of them had to resolve so he excused himself and left the room, closing the door behind him. Leaning back against it he closed his eyes, overwhelmed. The thought of Grace swollen with his child and Trace being a big brother had him thinking that he was the luckiest man in the world. He went down the stairs to find Cain's little boy Connor, who he knew was tormenting Walter.

~~~

"I have something to tell you. Something that I've never shared with anyone in my life," Grace told Trace when they were alone. "I'm telling you this so that you'll know just what you're going to be related to when I marry your dad. All right?"

"Yes. But if you think I'm going to let you go and run away then it won't work. I love you even if you send me away." Trace moved to lean against the headboard. "Are you going to have Dad's kid?"

"No. Not yet. We've never talked about having other children. Though I would like to, but it's a family decision, not just something that he and I can decide without your input. We're going to be a family, all three of us, and any other child that comes along."

She watched as he absorbed this. "Trace, what do you know about my parents?"

"Your dad is dead. Captain Grant killed him when he tried to kill your sister, Aunt Quinn. He was in prison for a long time and he…" He didn't finish, but looked at the empty fireplace.

"He killed someone. Yes, it's true. He was drunk and drove up on a sidewalk because the cars in front of him weren't going fast enough for him and he killed a man. My mother isn't any better."

Trace got up and sat on the footstool at her feet. "I heard Aunt Alyssa say that she was a peach. I don't think she meant the warm and fuzzy kind that Molly cuts up on my oatmeal."

Grace laughed. "No, she's not. She's…she's evil. Do you know what that word means?" He nodded, but she didn't wait for him to tell her. "My mother has split personalities. I've told your dad that. He also knows that she killed someone when I was a teenager. I didn't see her do it, but I knew that she had. Or at least one of the people she has in her head did it."

"She has people in her head that kill people? She's crazy then?" Trace reached out for her hand. "I'll protect you, Grace. I swear I won't let her hurt you."

"You have to stay away from them," she told him quickly. "There are several of them. I've met them all and they're dangerous. Promise me that you'll keep away from them."

"I will. I promise. What did she do to you, Grace? I know she hurt you. Tell me what she did to you."

Grace looked away from him, ashamed. She was ashamed for what she'd allowed her to do to her and, worse yet, let her get away with.

"She had someone rape me. She held me down while she…she encouraged my father to rape me." She still hadn't looked at the little boy in front of her. "I wasn't very old, seventeen. She'd tied me down after I'd been sleeping. I always thought she'd drugged me, but I couldn't remember. When I told her about it later, she'd acted like she had no idea." She was crying, the tears falling down her face hot and quick. When Trace said her name she didn't want

125

to look at him, didn't want to see the look on his face. When he said it a second time, she turned.

"I have a favor to ask you. I've been thinking about it for a long time. You can say no if you want to, but I'm not sure it'll keep me from doing it. Will you let me?"

She nodded.

"Will you please let me call you Mom?"

Grace stared at him for several seconds. He started talking again very quickly. "I've been thinking about it since that day you took me to the vet's for Walter. You were so brave when that kid threw that cat on that lizard. And when you told his mom to shut up and mind her tongue I about busted with love. She looked like she'd swallowed a bug. A big one. Then that nurse was starting on you." He laughed. "She backed up right away when you gave her that look. The one that said 'I'm not going to take your crap either, lady.' I still laugh about it sometimes."

"I'm not going to be a pushover with you either, you know. I'm going to expect you to be the worst little boy sometimes, and I might let you slide on some things, but then you'll be grounded when you need to be. And I'll want you to have a sick day from school even if you aren't sick; you'll have to help me plan stupid birthday parties for your dad and when we all have another baby, if we want, then I expect you to be big brother to it."

He looked like he was thinking about it then grinned at her. "Deal. But don't expect me to hug you in public. Grandma does it enough and I hate it." Then he grinned wider. "Not really, but I can't let her know that. She's my favorite grandma."

"Trace, I would be honored if you call me Mom. Just please don't call me Momma. I detest that stupid name."

"You got it, Momma."

Chapter 16

Joey looked at her stepson. Thomas had been a horror since the day she'd married his dad. And he hadn't improved one bit in all the years since. She supposed she should have put her foot down more, but the kid wouldn't listen to anyone. The few times that she had had to discipline him he'd rebelled so much and retaliated so harshly against the other children that she'd finally given up. She blamed herself for a little of what he'd done now.

She turned to the door when it opened. She burst into tears when she saw her husband and Michael walk in. Rushing to the men she was pulled into a tight hug and held. Sometimes, like now, a hug could make all the difference in the world. She was still crying when she pulled back.

"The nurse said that he'll be fine in a few days and the police are going to take him to the infirmary at the jail. They thought about leaving him here, but they just don't have the manpower." She looked over at Thomas who was cuffed to the bed by his ankle and wrist. "I'm actually afraid for him. He killed one of their own and I know they aren't too thrilled about the fact that he survived whoever shot him."

"Have they figured out what happened yet? Payton said that he was screaming about being framed for those two men, that a woman had actually committed the crimes."

Joey knew from Michael's tone that he didn't believe his stepbrother, not that she blamed him.

"They didn't say, but then I doubt very much they would tell us. They took both bodies to the coroner's office to see what they could find. I did hear that both of them died about the same time and that one had been cut up, the other stabbed through the heart." Joey sat down on the couch next to Michael as she continued. "They have him for the other two murders, so I don't suppose they care one way or the other if he killed these two or not."

Joey glanced over at the cop she'd forgotten about. He'd not left the room since Thomas had been brought back from surgery. She wondered if he would save Thomas if someone, the supposed woman, came back to finish the job. She doubted it. She also doubted that she would care all that much either. The thought made her feel like a horrible person and she felt more tears fall. Before she could say anything Lucas started talking.

"The older man was the super of the apartment complex where he died. They aren't sure what the connection was, only that he had been stabbed in the heart and that he had a blunt force to the back of his head. They are doing a room to room search to see if he was killed there. The younger man had been cut badly. They said that he'd been wrapped in plastic and put down there first because he was beneath the older man. He'd been stored down there for at least twenty-four hours." The cop coughed, but didn't speak as her husband continued. "There are seventy-two apartments in that complex and most of the people are...less than trustworthy. I understand that any one of the residents there could have killed either man as it seems to be a regular occurrence in that neighborhood."

"Four to five per week," the cop said. "We get a call there four, sometimes as many as ten times a week for one thing or another. The man, the younger one, he's a known prostitute in the area about three blocks from there. And the kid here is going to trial. It's a capital to kill a cop in this state."

Joey shuddered. The death penalty was almost a guarantee for Thomas. She looked at him again before she spoke to the cop. "Did

128

you know him; the other policeman, did you know him? And did he have a family? I'm not sure…my family would like to make a donation to whatever fund you have for them. And I know you'll keep that to yourself.'

He nodded. "Officer Bill Abbott, ma'am. And Officer Tyler and I will. I know…your husband is a good man, fair too. I was before him on a few cases."

Joey smiled as she looked at her husband. He'd been a sitting judge for a few years before they'd married and he'd become a well-known and very well respected circuit court judge before he'd retired. He still presided over some cases when needed, filling in for vacations or some other thing, but he'd been retired for a few years now.

Thomas stirred and they all looked at the bed expectantly. The doctor had told them that he would be out for a bit, but when he came around they would make sure that he could move about before sending him on his way. They'd been told they could stay with him until then, but after being transported he was going to be in lock down. Mostly, they'd been told, for his own safety.

The bullet had entered his right arm. The doctor who had treated him said that it had gone through his bicep. He said that it hadn't been anywhere near as life threatening as the person who had called it in had said and he'd wondered to them if it was a lover's quarrel and that she'd had remorse over trying to kill him. Thomas had been awake when they'd brought him in and, at that time, they hadn't discovered the bodies. Nor, it seemed, had they realized who they had. It wasn't until he was transported that they made the connection to him and the cop killer at his home. By then Thomas had already been taken to surgery.

"Dad? Where…what am I doing here?" Thomas pulled on the cuff at his wrist. "What the fuck is this? Why am I…am I in trouble for something? That bitch shot me and you have me in cuffs? I want these things taken off me right fucking now."

"Shut up, you little prick," Michael said softly. "You're lucky that you're not in prison, you fool. What the fuck did you think was going to happen? That they'd throw a parade in your honor? You killed the senator's daughter, you spoiled little bastard."

"I didn't kill anyone who didn't deserve it. And who the hell do you think you are talking to me like I'm subhuman? You have a dead hooker on your lawn. What the hell is your precious Grace going to think about marrying you now, huh? And that little bastard of yours? What do you—"

Officer Brent Tyler was standing over him with his baton out and at his throat before any of them could move. Michael put his hand on his shoulder and the man seemed to ripple with anger. Joey was suddenly very afraid for his stepson.

"Officer Tyler, let him go," Michael said calmly. "He's not worth it. I know what you're thinking, but he isn't worth losing your job over. He's been a selfish little prick all his life."

Joey looked at her husband as he backed away. She couldn't tell what he was thinking, but she had a pretty good idea. He was blaming himself, as she was doing. He was thinking just like her and that, if they had done more, maybe none of this would be happening.

"He can't say things like that. We have him…there is a tape that shows him killing that girl. That little girl was seventeen." Officer Tyler pulled back, but not before he put a bit more pressure on Thomas throat. "But you're right, Mr. Cunningham, he just ain't worth it. Nobody's worth the death of a cop killer who is going to get the chair anyway."

Before Thomas could open his mouth his father stepped back to the bed. "Shut the fuck up before I let this man shoot you."

They all moved away from the bed. Thomas glared, but thankfully kept his mouth shut. The nurse came in twice; once to check on his IV, the next time to bring him a tray with clear liquids. Thomas took one look at the broth and other things on the tray and shoved the entire thing, including the half table, away. Anger practically boiled off him as he glared at Michael. Joey thought, if given the chance, Thomas would kill Michael without any qualms. But she was sure that, given Michael's background, Thomas would be dead before he got close enough.

~~~

Ginny locked the door behind her. They'd had to move and move quickly. The fucking bitch Verrie had nearly gotten them all caught. What the hell was she thinking bringing her "work," as she called it, to where they lived? And now, now they were back in Ohio.

The dive was just that, a dive. The walls had water stains running down them that looked as if the bathtub upstairs had overflowed and poured down the walls. That might have been believable it this hadn't been but a one-story complex and the only thing above them was the open sky. The bathroom, not much bigger than a shoebox, had a shower stall and a toilet. The sink was so close to the toilet that you could literally reach all the way across it to the door knob. The floor was cracked tile that was in an undetermined color and she was sure it hadn't seen either mop or cleaning agents since the place was built. But what the floor lacked in color, the walls and the shower curtain certainly made up for.

The curtain was puce. A shade so ugly that, if you were feeling any sort of upset stomach, would certainly make you toss your belly. The sink was green, a lime green that made your eyes ache. The tub and the toilet a muddy brown that was probably due more to the state of its lack of cleanliness than a manufacturer's idea of a color. Ginny only hoped that if the need for a shower came up soon it would be dark out so that she could do it without the light on.

The bedroom wasn't much better in either cleanness or color. The picture over the bed of a naked woman with a simple apple over her pussy was the least offensive part of the room. The spread was covered in bugs and she was hoping it was the pattern and not real ones. She hadn't looked under it, not even sure she wanted to see the sheets. The pillows, if there were any, were the same thickness as the spread and probably just as buggy. She sat in the bright orange chair and closed her eyes. What the fuck was she doing here?

She wasn't aware when they'd fled New York. Thankfully someone, one of the others, had known where to find everything they'd needed to get a plane ticket and get them to safety. Ginny wasn't even sure what had happened other than she had shot someone and that the person had discovered her body. She didn't know anything else. But what she did know, or had guessed, was that the police thought someone else had done the deeds and not her.

"They will find out it wasn't him. When they do, Grace is going to kill us."

Ginny looked in the mirror at Guinnie. She wasn't strong enough to speak to her through a simple mind connection, so Ginny spoke to her this way. "You're just a kid; what the hell do you know about it? And where have you been? Did one of the others hurt you?" Guinnie was shaking her head before Ginny finished the question. "Why do you think Grace is going to kill us? She only knows us as her mother."

"No, she doesn't. I told her about us."

Ginny's eyes widened in the reflection.

"She knows more than any of the other children because I liked her most. Grace would talk to me when the others walked away. She saw Verrie kill a man at her home."

Ginny felt her heart pound. Grace knew and, worse yet, she knew that Verrie had a bad habit. Trying to remain calm so that she wouldn't alert the others, she looked back at Guinnie when she realized she was talking.

"You aren't the host. You never were. I know that Verrie told you that, but she lied. Verrie is the host." The sing-song voice was irritating. And Ginny knew that she knew it. "The others, they think that they are the host as well. She tells them all."

Ginny rubbed her forehead. "Why? What possible reason could she have for lying to us all? And why would she want us to think we were the ones in charge? Don't you think it would benefit her best if she was the one…"

"Yes, that's it. Or so I've heard. She wants you all to fight about yourselves. If you fight, she can control us. I want this to end. I'm…I'm still a little girl because I can't grow and she will not let me."

Ginny heard the anger in her voice, but was too busy trying to figure out Verrie's angle. She got up to pace. She could still see

Guinnie, but only in small glimpses that showed a small child of about ten or so. Ginny knew that she'd been there all along. She'd only come out when the children, Guinevere's kids, needed her. And now. She started to ask her why she was here now when something else occurred to her.

"Will Grace tell them what she knows? Will she, you think, tell her family about us?"

Guinnie nodded.

"This isn't good. This will get us put away and I don't want that to happen. No way are they going to lock my happy ass up."

"Or they will kill us." She sounded so wishful that Ginny stopped to stare. "You have to admit that we are not doing so great. If we continue to fight, then we will destroy each other anyway."

Ginny had been thinking the same thing, but it didn't set well with her to have it pointed out to her by a child. She glared at Guinnie and decided that she'd had enough of Miss Doom and Gloom. She turned her back on her and tried to bring Guinevere to her. The laughter behind her made her think of nails on a chalk board and metal against her fillings. She turned slowly.

"I'm neither as weak as you think, nor am I as easily dismissed. I may look like a child to you, but I've been around as long as you. I listen and pay attention." Pain seared through Ginny's head as Guinnie continued. "You'd do well to remember that without me, you would be nothing."

Ginny felt dizziness swamp her and she felt the floor come up to grab her. Her last thought was that she hoped the floor was cleaner than it smelled before she heard the other two, Guinevere and Verrie, scream.

Chapter 17

Thomas looked around the room again. He was waiting for his chance, and the man who'd taken his blood pressure an hour ago said when it came, he had to be ready. The gun lying beside him made him feel that he'd be able to do just about anything. And the fact that the man had opened each of the cuffs before he'd left was amazing to Thomas. The fire alarm nearly startled him into a stupor. He pulled his hand free as soon as the cop stepped out of the room.

Thomas hid behind the door and waited. His arm was throbbing, but he was about to be set free so, he thought, as soon as he could he'd get himself something to take care of it and to help him deal with the stress of this shit. As soon as the door started to open Thomas tensed, ready to take out who ever came in. He was thrilled when he saw it was Michael.

He hit him three times with the gun, twice in the head. Michael was down after the second time, but he hit him again for good measure. The blood that was spilling from his stepbrother's head made him giddy with power, so Thomas kicked him twice in the ribs because he could. Stepping over his body, Thomas moved to the slightly opened door to see the cop coming toward him. Instead of bolting like he wanted to do he pulled back into the room and waited.

As soon as the prick walked through the door Thomas hit him too. He didn't want to waste any more time so he took the cop's gun, phone, and radio and left the room. He was nearly to the elevator when he realized he should have put on something more than the stupid gown he had on. Thomas slipped into the first room he came to and was glad it appeared to be a man's room. After going through the suitcase he'd found still laying on the bed, he went into the bathroom and changed.

The clothes were cheap and ill-fitting but so much better than the gown he'd had on. He tried to adjust them to fit him better, but he couldn't seem to get it right. He was going to leave the name of his tailor, but decided that he'd better get moving. The shoes fit, but again were cheap and well-worn.

He was about to leave when he noticed that a purse was lying there alongside of a wallet and keys. Knowing that he had to get away before he was noticed, he grabbed up the wallet and the keys. While he was stuffing the wallet away he rummaged through the purse until he found cash. Seventy bucks was all he could find, but it was better than nothing. Going out the door, he was out of the building when he heard the alarms sound. Christ, he was finally free.

The car was just where the man said it was, but Thomas walked by it. He was actually a little nervous about accepting help from someone he didn't know. Not to mention, every time he'd asked him why, the "nurse" would change the subject. He used the automatic unlock on the keys he'd stolen to find the other car. He heard the beep just as he saw the man who'd helped him.

Nurse was standing next to a lamp post with three other men. Thomas was beginning to think he'd been set up. Opening the gun for the first time, he found it was empty and that the clip in the boot of it held nothing more than air. Thomas leaned heavily against his new ride and thought of the implications of what had just happened.

Whoever "helped" him wanted him to get into some sort of shootout with the cops. And with the gun he'd been given they fully expected him to die. Taking out the cop's gun, he checked it. Loaded and one in the barrel. Walking toward the car that had been provided for him to get away with, Thomas smiled at the men. By the time he was ten feet away he lifted his gun and shot all four of them with the cop's gun. Hurrying over to them before anyone noticed the blood or called the real cops because of the noise he took each of their weapons and wallets.

Sitting in the stolen car he took all the cash he'd stolen and put it on the seat beside him. He now had just over nine hundred dollars in cash, three Glocks, and two revolvers. He pulled out of the lot, trying to think where to go. He decided that it was time to pay the bitch who he felt had started this all with a little visit. By the time he got to the Washington building he had a plan and he was a happy man.

But pulling up in front of the building made him pissed all over again. Cunningham Construction was moving shit out. He wasn't sure what had happened. He had only just found out the Washington building belonged to Grace a couple of days before. The fact that Grace owned it didn't really surprise him; it was the fact that no one had bothered to tell him that she did. He felt, as a Cunningham too, he should be privy to the entire goings on of the company. He frowned when he realized why he might not have been told, but someone might have said something.

Thomas thought about going over and seeing if he could find out where she was. On the off chance that one of the peons might have a clue, he nearly had the door opened when he saw one of the guys from the office he sort of knew. Thomas thought maybe he was some mail clerk, but didn't really care enough to waste much time on trying to figure it out. He slipped up beside him when he wasn't paying attention. The man jumped when he noticed Thomas.

"Where are we taking all this stuff? I thought I was supposed to be here now, but I guess someone had the times wrong about when we were supposed to show up." Thomas leaned against the car and smiled. "I've been working on some other project and forgot I was supposed to be here for my brother." He hated referring to Michael as anything but his stepbrother. He loathed the man and everything he stood for. He told himself all the time that had he been the son of the new squeeze, he would have gotten all his father's attention too. Thomas resented anything that came from Michael and hated that he called himself Cunningham.

"Supposed to be taking this to the main offices. Mr. Cunningham said we were to unpack it just like we packed it up. Even had us taking pictures of her stuff so we could set it up just the same. I guess she's some sort of dressmaker." The man said it like he was impressed.

"That's right. I forgot." Thomas snapped his fingers like he'd just remembered. "I'm having a brain fart of a day. Grace wanted me to call her when things were starting to get set up. I can't seem to find the number she gave me. I don't suppose you know where she might be, do you?"

"Yeah, she's in Ohio with her family. Heard tell that they went there for a visit or something. Might be popping the question any day now is what I heard."

Thomas shuddered to think about a dressmaker being in his family as the man continued.

"If you wanna be the one to call her, you'll have to find the number from Mason. He's over there near the truck."

Thomas nodded and stood up. "Thanks. I'll just go and see him now. Might get me in better with my brother if I call her and tell her that things are moving the way Michael said. She is a might bitchy when things don't go her way." Thomas laughed and walked toward Mason. He kept to the side of the truck as Mason directed things being loaded in the moving van. Thomas needed him to be alone and, the sooner he could get him there, the better. But luck was on his side. Mason was called away and, when he put his clipboard down on one of the chairs and walked away, Thomas walked up and took it off the seat.

"There you are," he said as he found the address. Taking off the top sheet he stuffed it in his pocket and, after tossing the clipboard back on the seat, he walked away quickly. Like he was concerned about where her shit was. As far as he was concerned she was going to be a widow, long before she was associated with his family for very long.

~~~

"The doctor said I'm going to be fine. As soon as he clears me I'm coming back. My parents are coming with me and we'll all sit down and talk about this mess."

Grace wiped at the tears. "I'm so sorry he hurt you. I wish I could be there for you." She looked over at Trace as he sat staring at her from the other chair. "Trace said you'd be all right. He seems to think you have a hard noodle."

"I do. Tell him I'm fine. He worries as much as my mother. I'm going to be home by nightfall. Then I want to find you in that big house and make love to you several times."

She grinned at the phone as he continued.

"At least you'll know that I will never complain about a headache when you want to jump my bones someday."

She tried not to think about making love with him whenever she wanted. He simply made her melt like she was an ice cube on the sidewalk in mid-July. Glancing over at Trace she decided to change the subject. "I've set up a meeting with my family. I...if you're not here I'm going to start without you. It's time they knew everything." Grace knew that she should have told them any number of times she'd been home over the years, but just couldn't bring herself to do it. "Cain is worried I'm going to tell them I'm pregnant. I assured him that I'm not."

"Do you want to be? Pregnant, I mean. I know we haven't really talked much, but I'd like to have a child or several with you. The thought of you big with my baby makes me smile like a sap."

Grace glanced at Trace before she answered. "We'll all need to talk about that, including Trace. If we're going to be a family then we'll need to make those decisions as one too." She lowered her voice enough so that only Michael could hear. "He thinks I'm going to send him away when you and I have a child. I couldn't do that to any of us."

"It happened to his buddy," he told her just as quietly. "We'll talk more when I get there. The doctor is here now. I'll call you from the airport. I have a car already here, ready to get me there."

After telling her he loved her and she him, they hung up. Trace looked at her with a smile. She was beginning to think that was all he did and it made her feel good.

"He's leaving the hospital soon. He'll call from the airport. He should be here very soon." She laughed when he nodded. "What is it? Are you so bored with being my protector that you have nothing to say to your dad coming home?"

"No. I was thinking about what you said about talking to your family. Are you scared?" he asked her. "I would be. I'd be really scared they'd be mad at me."

"I am. A little anyway. They're not going to be very happy with me for not telling them. But I've..." Grace took a deep breath. "Trace, if you ever need me, ever to just talk or anything, I want you to know that I'm here."

He got up and came to her. "I know that. And Grace, why don't you and I go tell them together? I'll have your back and if they give you any crap, I'll...I'll tell my grandma and she'll kick their butts for them."

Grace laughed and pulled him to her lap. She was so in love with this little guy that she ached from it. She kissed his forehead and laughed again at his groan. Watching him become a man was going to be a blast.

They entered the room that had been set up to accommodate them all with snacks a few minutes later. Connor had wanted to take Trace to his playroom, but he said he wanted to stay with her. She assured him she'd be fine. After a few more tugs on his arm Trace went with her nephew and closed the door behind him.

"Nothing you have to tell us is as bad as you look like it might be," Cain told her as he sat down. "We all love you very much and whatever it is, we'll work it out. I swear."

Grace nodded. "I know that, but...I guess I should start at the beginning. And before you interrupt me after I start, I know that I should have...I know that I should have told you before. Before all of this started happening, before I left home, and long before..." She took a deep breath. "Mother has split personalities. Several, as a matter of fact. I've been in cont—"

140

"Wait. You can't just jump in like that and expect us not to have questions." Quinn looked around the room as she continued. "We all know she's a little off, but split personalities? The next thing you're going to say is that she is the one who has been killing all the people surrounding us and has been the one who tried to have us kidnapped."

"She is," Payton said quietly. "We didn't know about the personality disorder, but the rest, we figured it out a few days ago. She's also the one who has been stealing the money from Alyssa and Cain's account."

Quinn got up and jerked away from Drew when he tried to pull her back. "No. She can't have killed anyone. You're wrong. If she is the one who... Oh my God, are you saying that she is the one who shot Payton, the one who tried to... No, I won't believe it. A mother just wouldn't do those things. Not to her own child."

"You knew," Sin said as she watched Quinn. "You knew, didn't you? You knew what she was too and you didn't say anything thing either."

"I don't know what you're talking about," Quinn said as she began pacing the room. "You're all wrong. It was just a fluke of the lighting that's all. I didn't see anything."

"I saw her too," Jazzie said suddenly. "The day I was kidnapped from the restaurant. I remember thinking it was her, but I...she was different. More...aggressive, I guess. I remember thinking that she was younger looking and more put together too."

"That would have been Ginny. Their names are Ginny, Guinnie, Verrie, and of course, Mother. Ginny is the thinker. She's also the most organized. Verrie is violent. She is the one who murders, and Guinnie is...she's a child. I would say if she hasn't grown up over the years, she's about ten or so." Grace started to reach for a glass of tea and noticed her hands were shaking so she dropped them back in her lap. "I spoke to Guinnie more than the others. She's the one who made me understand what was happening."

"Maybe you should start from the beginning. Start with the first time you talked to...did you say her name was Guinnie?" Shamus

141

grinned. "Their names, they're all just variations on Guinevere's, aren't they?"

Grace shuddered. Yes, she knew that because Guinnie had told her that they were all a part of the whole so they had to share the one name. She looked up at her brother-in-law and began. "I was six and father had just beaten me with an orange race track thing that boys race their cars on. Mother was in the kitchen and…"

She talked until Michael called and said that he'd landed at the Columbus Airport.

Chapter 18

Verrie waited until the gates closed before she shot the driver of the limo. He was useless now anyway, so she simply opened the door to the limo on the way up to the main house and rolled him out. He was just one less person she had to deal with in a long line of fuck ups. Starting the limo again, she smiled at her good fortune.

She'd been trying to figure out how to get to the house and where they all were since yesterday. Cain and the money-grubbing whore had the place locked down like they had all of Fort Knox in there instead of a bunch of brats and her target. Time to fucking end this shit. She slowed as she approached the house and sneered at what Ginny thought of as the most beautiful house she'd ever seen.

The fucking others were starting to get on her nerves too. Especially Guinnie. That kid was the first order of business when this was over. She and the others had been pandering to her childlike stupidity since day one and it was time for her to grow up or shut the fuck up.

Verrie frowned when she thought about the things she'd found out yesterday. The simple fact that Guinnie had been telling on them to the girl, Grace, for all these years was bad enough, but her knowing that she was lying about the host scared her just a little. How the fuck did she know?

And how did she get to talk to the children when they hadn't been aware? Verrie had asked the other two and, not only did they

143

not know, but they'd been surprised that anyone other than them knew about the others. Grace knowing made them have to step up their game and end her. Grace wasn't just a means to the money and other things they would get when they were all dead, but she was a liability too.

But, now, she was going to finish this. In fact, it had been with Ginny and Guinevere's blessing to kill Grace first. She smiled when she thought of the conversation she'd had with them yesterday, marveling that they could as easily block out Guinnie as she'd been doing to them for all these years. Verrie stopped the limo that was to take Grace to the airport to pick up the bastard and thought about it.

"She knows how much, I wonder? I mean, does she know everything or just...fuck, when I think of all the shit she could know, it makes me want to find her and kill her right fucking now." Verrie had been pacing in the filthy apartment they'd found in an abandoned complex. "She could know nothing, but she could know everything."

Verrie had a long list of things that Grace could know. None of them very good. In fact, most of them would get her the chair or worse. She couldn't stand the thought of being locked away for the rest of her life. They'd drug them all up and she didn't want to think about not being able to have sex the way she'd grown to love.

"Any one of us could get into trouble if she knew only half of what we've done. Even you, Guinevere. Think of all the shit you've done to your precious little brats." Ginny laughed when Guinevere huffed. "Oh you know that you hate them. Why the fuck else would you have named them such ridiculous names? And for as much as I want to fuck that son of yours, there ain't no way I'm going to go to some institution for it. Fuck that shit."

Guinevere huffed again. "I never wanted them in the first place. My Roscoe told me that I had to get in the family way and when they were born, they'd take care of us in our golden years. Now look. He's dead and I can't get my only son to provide for me. It's all that money-grubbing whore's fault; every single thing that has gone wrong can be traced back to her and her ways. I think we should just kill her and get it over with. No more fucking around with those girls. They're pretty useless anyway."

Verrie agreed, but she didn't say anything. She was trying to make sure that Guinnie didn't move in on their conversation. She didn't feel her there and every time she'd asked the other two, they hadn't either, but Verrie was sure the fucking shit had been listening. And now they had a plan. Take Grace out and, once she was out, get the rest of them at her funeral. They even knew someone who could make a bomb big enough to take out everyone at the burial. *Bang!* No more kids, no more grandkiddies and, best of all, no more issues.

She settled back to wait. Verrie had heard the guy on the intercom tell her, who he thought was the driver, that the miss would be out directly, to wait for her to come out. *Sure,* Verrie thought, *and I'll fucking tote her fucking ass out of here too.* She looked down at the gun and knife on the seat. *Yeah, I'm going to enjoy this.*

The kid coming out was a surprise. Verrie had never seen this one before and realized he was probably the man's brat. Michael Cunningham, she thought his name was, and grinned when she thought about the two for one she was getting. Then he simply hugged Grace and turned and went back into the house. She closed up the window between the seats and started the car again as soon as the door closed. They were pulling out of the long drive when Verrie's phone went off. She simply slid the thing to go straight to voicemail.

Traffic was light this time of the evening she realized. Verrie knew from the conversation she'd had with the driver that they were going to the airport and that they were picking up some people from a private airstrip. Money again, and Verrie knew that if she had the time she'd take whoever got off the plane, cut them to pieces, and spread them all over the front lawn. But she couldn't, not yet. The plan had to be followed or it would be bad for them all. But getting into the gated area was where they'd fallen short on ideas. Then she'd happened upon a solution by trying to hire a limo to take her to the house.

She'd found the driver at the Ride in Style limo service. In fact, she'd met him once or twice before when some event had the family using the same service for events. She'd tried to remember his name when she'd walked up to him earlier and had it not been for his name badge, she wouldn't have had a clue. But Bob had been very happy to see her and more than happy to give her a ride to the "big house" when her own car had broken down.

"Can't have the boss's mom walking back to the 'big house' now, can we? You just hop your little self inside of that cool ride and I'll take you to the front door." She wanted to throw up at his flirty ways, but simply smiled and got into the front. They were on their way when he told her he was to pick up Grace and take her to the airport to get her man. "They seem like a nice couple. Took them both to the house with his little boy when they landed yesterday. Real polite kid. Didn't get stuff all over the seats like some of those rich people's brats do when they ride. Nope, sat there talking to his daddy and Miss Grace like a real good boy."

Like she cared, but nodded all the same. Verrie hated kids. They were messy, loud, and couldn't have a single function that she could think of that made them worth nine months of being a cow and then years of putting up with their shit. Then to have them turn on you...well, that shit was going to be laid to rest right now. They were pulling off the main road when she thought of how much fun she was going to have.

~~~

Grace was exhausted. After talking with her family for over three hours and then the tense fight she'd had with Trace she just wanted to close her eyes and sleep for several days. The frantic call from her employees made her grind her teeth. The nerve of the man moving her offices into his building and not telling her. They were going to have a nice long...conversation when he got back.

Margo had called to say that her office wasn't set up and the redecorators weren't listening to her. They were hanging the pictures in the wrong order and the mural she'd made wasn't among the things they'd packed up.

"What decorator and what office? Take a deep breath and tell me what's going on." Grace had closed the door to Cain's office to speak to her in private. "What do you mean my mural isn't among the packed things? Who is packing things and why?"

"Michael came by with some guy the other day. He said that we were moving to another building and he said you knew."

She knew she was moving, but thought it was to a storage shed, not to some place that had an office.

"The place is awesome, by the way. We even have off street parking and there's a cafeteria on the second floor that—"

"Focus, Margo. What is going on? Why are our things being put away in a building?" Grace's head hurt even after an hour of talking to her. "Tell me where we're moved to."

An hour later, she still didn't have a clue where her mural was because Margo had gone back to the warehouse to look for it. It had been sandblasted off the walls, she'd said. As was, she went on to tell her, most of the floors on the main level. The men had gotten to work on the building the moment the last piece of her business had been moved out.

Grace pulled out the sheet of paper of things she was going to talk to Michael about and the first was doing things without her being aware of them. She might have had some say in the move if for no other reason than to tell him she appreciated it. The limo driving over a particularly hard bump had her bumping her head on the window she was next to. Grace looked out the window and her skin dampened with terror.

They were no longer on the highway on their way to the airport. She had no idea where they were, but she was now sure that something was wrong. She pulled out her cell phone and dialed Michael's number when the window between her and the driver slid down and a gun appeared.

"Hello, Grace. I'm Verrie, and you and I are going to have a bit of a talk and then I'm going to kill you."

Grace slid her cell phone to the seat as soon as the window whined as it rolled down. She didn't even look to see if anyone answered, but hoped that someone had. "I know who you are. You

147

and the others are about to get your asses handed to you." Verrie waved the gun and Grace moved to the middle of the seat as indicated before continuing. "My brother is looking for you right now with a bunch of agents and cops. You won't get away—"

"Shut the fuck up," Verrie snapped. "You have no idea what you've done. And even if they did know about where we were you're still gonna be dead. And at the lovely funeral, your poor mother won't be able to attend because she'll be so heartbroken that she'll be in the hospital when the entire entourage is killed in a massive explosion. All of you will be dead and we'll have it all as sole survivors."

Grace threw back her head and laughed. "You think it's going to be that easy to kill me? Think again, bitch. I'm armed too." The gun slide out of her purse and was in her hand in seconds. She was glad to see the shocked look on her face. "Now put down the gun, Verrie, before I have to kill the lot of you. Not that anyone will miss you all, but I really would like for you to stand trial."

The gun went off, narrowly missing Grace. She felt the wind shear her cheek as it whizzed by. Then, for only a second, Verrie froze. That was when Grace knew she was looking at someone else.

"Run," the voice said. "Hurry, run."

Grace knew who it was before she moved to the door to go. Guinnie was helping her escape. Grace was glad; she really wasn't sure she could have killed the woman who was basically her mother, but she would if she had to. She was out of the car and running for her life when she felt the first bullet tear through her arm. The laughter coming from behind her made the hair on her neck rise, and her to stumble from terror. She'd forgotten her phone too.

Crawling to the fallen tree, she could hear someone running up behind her quickly. She wasn't sure she could make it, but when the person went by her she felt she might be safe long enough to catch her breath and to look at her arm. It was throbbing like a toothache and she wanted to scream every time she touched it.

It wasn't until she was sure she wasn't going to bleed to death that she started to sit up. She was glad she'd worn her dark pants

148

and jacket, because the moon was nearly nonexistent and she didn't want to die out here in the middle of nowhere. She could make out the shiny car from the stars and decided that if she could get to her phone she might be able to call for help. Her gun had dropped when she'd gotten shot and even if she had a way to find it she was right-handed and had never been able to make her left shoot worth a damn. Closing her eyes, she decided that if she lived through this, she was going to make Sin teach her how to shoot the sucker with her toes if she thought she could learn it. The slight noise to her left had her opening her eyes and straining hard to see who was there.

Verrie walked by her without a sound. Grace might have been impressed if she wasn't so terrified. The woman didn't make a single sound that would have let her know who was coming. Then another voice, this one chilling, made her nearly whimper.

"Did you find her yet? You said I could fuck her when you brought her here. What the fuck happened?" Thomas was here as well.

"Shhhh, you fucking moron. I'm still looking for her. And when I find her I'm going to fucking empty my clip in her. Fucking bitch was a lot faster than I thought she'd be."

She didn't know, was Grace's first thought. She either didn't know about Guinnie at all or just that she'd helped Grace escape. She thought it highly unlikely that she didn't know about Guinnie when Grace knew about them, but she was glad for the younger girl's help.

149

Kathi S. Barton

150

Chapter 19

Michael collapsed. He'd heard the voices seconds before he'd answered her then, while he was trying to motion for someone to come and help him, he'd heard the gunshot. He held the phone to his ear, trying to hear anything as his father came toward him.

"Someone has Grace. I think it might be Verrie. I have to…call the house. Tell them everything I say." Michael tried to work around the lump in his throat. "Ask them if Trace is there or if he is with Grace and to come and get me."

He heard his father talking, but was trying hard to hear anything going on at the other end of Grace's phone. There was another shot, this one farther away, but nothing more. Then, as his father turned to him, he thought he heard Thomas.

"It's Cain. He wants to know if she has the same cell phone as before. He said that Shamus has a tracker on it and that they're headed to it now. And Trace is with someone named Alyssa."

Michael nodded.

"The cops are on their—"

Michael held up his hand when he heard something and his father closed his mouth with a snap.

"…care what you think. You fucking moron. If you want to fuck her, you'll have to do it after I kill her. She's caused me enough fucking problems to last four lifetimes."

151

"I'm not fucking her dead. And I want her awake when it happens. If you so much as put another bullet in her before I get my chance then I'll...I'll kill you."

Michael looked at his dad as he stood in front of him as Thomas spoke. He covered the mouth piece and took a pen from his pocket as he pinched the phone between his shoulder and chin. He wrote the word "Thomas" on his hand, and nodded when Lucas looked up at him sharply.

He heard something thud, then more cussing. He heard someone moan and knew it was Grace. At least she was still alive was all he could think about. Then more doors slamming before the car started. This time when someone spoke it was muffled. He couldn't make out much, only an occasional word here and there, but not enough to figure out who the woman was and what she was doing with Grace. He had a pretty good idea, but nothing concrete.

When Lucas handed him his cell phone and his mom and he walked away Michael held the phone to his other ear and said hello.

"We've pinpointed the area where she is by less than ten feet. It would be better if she hadn't taken her out in the middle of nowhere, but we know close enough...fuck," Payton snapped. "They're on the move. Could be better this way. They might move into somewhere we can get a better bead on them."

"Grace is still alive. I can hear them. Thomas is with them. He's...he wants her. The woman she's with is saying things that... From what Grace has told me, it could be Verrie, the one who killed the man in her parents' house when she was a kid."

Payton would know better than anyone not to give him platitudes or soft words. Like his business dealings, he was more of a "give it to me straight" kind of guy. So he was very grateful for Payton in his next words.

"She can hold her own, but this woman is beyond nuts. We've been doing some investigating since you and I've talked and we're reasonably sure she's responsible for nearly all the killings that have been associated with the family. And I've had a buddy of mine doing some looking around on the family property, both here and in California." Payton paused just enough that Michael knew he wasn't going to like what he said next. "They've been able to uncover at least four bodies here and one in Cali. Two of those here haven't been in the ground long, the other as recent as the last year. The one they've been able to see has been mutilated. We're waiting on word to see if it was post or during."

Michael had a feeling that they would find she'd done it while the guy was still living. He shuddered when he thought of what could happen to Grace. The limo pulled up in front of him and slid to a soft stop. He turned his back to it and spoke to Payton again. "Did you send us a car?" Payton said he had and gave him the driver information. "All right. My parents and I are coming there. Tell Trace…tell him we'll get her back and that I'll be there soon."

"Will do," Payton said. "And Michael, when this is over, I'd like to talk to you about moving here permanently. You and the new family can build and we'll be all one big, happy clan."

Michael didn't say anything. His throat had closed up on the emotion he felt about having a family of his own. He sat in the limo across from the only father he'd ever known and didn't know what to say to him. He was glad that the man seemed to know this and didn't speak either for a long time.

"It's entirely my fault," Lucas said and before Michael could tell him he was full of shit he raised his hand to stop him. "Just after his mother died I sort of went into a deep sort of depression. He was hurting too, I guess. Though to be honest, I never really thought that Thomas knew his mother all that well. He'd been in trouble a great deal as a child and we ended up having him put…away, I guess. He'd had this…he would kill the neighbor's animals. Just for fun, he'd told us. It was just a way to pass the time."

"How old was he?" Joey asked softly. "How old was he when it started and then when he was let go?"

They both looked at Lucas as he shifted on his seat. "Five. His mother died when he was seven so he was in the home for just under two years. And when he came home he was so different. And as long as he took his medications he was the same as every other little boy."

153

Michael waited and when Lucas didn't speak for a while he reached over and took his hand. "What happened to make you not want to be with him anymore? What made you turn from him?"

Lucas turned and looked at him with tears in his eyes. Michael could see the pain there. It was raw and open, nearly as messy as a real wound and no less painful.

"I fell in love with your mother and you. You were the kind of son I wanted. Normal and smart. You seemed to have it all together and knew just what you wanted, what you needed. And then when you signed up for the service I realized that I loved you more than I ever had Thomas and would never feel…I'm such a horrible man."

The sobs tore through Michael. He didn't know what to do about what Lucas had just said, so he looked to his mother. She, too, was crying, but her tears were silent. She held onto her husband and said soft words, but nothing that Michael could understand.

"You're not a horrible man. And I'll kill anyone who tries to say differently." Michael looked away as he began telling his parents something he'd never told anyone before. "Thomas was…he's evil. He's always been that way, even when we were children. I knew about things, things that I'd never talked about with you, but I learned to watch out for. Things like people around him. He always acted, no matter who they were, that he was above them. And the drugs didn't help him either."

"Drugs?" Lucas asked. "I never… Well, I suppose that's not true either. He seemed to be fine for long periods and, though I should have questioned him, to be honest I was just glad he wasn't bothering me. And the evil part, I agree. As much as it pains me to say it, he should never have been released from that home. None of this would have happened if I had just—"

"Thomas is with someone who is by far more insane than him. You remember me telling you about Grace's mother? Well, she has her too. And Thomas is with them. I don't know what the outcome will be, but the Feds are involved and so are the locals. He killed a cop, Dad. They aren't going to go easy on him when they find him."

154

Lucas nodded. "No. And I hate to say this, but he's finally getting what he deserves. He's been doing things to lead up to this his entire life."

The rest of the ride was made in silence. Michael wanted his Grace back. He wanted to take her to the big bedroom they'd shared the night before he'd been called back and make love to her until neither of them could walk. He wanted children with her, lots of them so that Trace would be a big brother. As soon as they pulled into the drive of the mansion his son came running out of the house and hugged him tight.

"They found a dead man at the end of the drive. Aunt Alyssa said this place is becoming a battle ground."

Michael picked him up and was glad that he didn't protest.

"Aunt Sin said as soon as I'm old enough she's going to teach me how to use a machine gun. She said that way I can protect us all when they get too old to do it themselves."

Michael looked up at the woman in question and she waved. He was going to have to have a talk with the little woman before she had Trace as scary as she was. He nodded before he spoke to Trace. "You might want to take that up with Grace. She might have a few things to say about that too." Trace scrambled down and walked with him to the house. "Have they heard anything?"

Michael had lost the connection with the call not long after they'd gotten in the limo. He had called Payton and he'd told him that they still had a bead on the phone and that he would call him as soon as there was anything different. The closer Michael got to the steps, the more worried he got. Something had happened and he was sure it wasn't good news.

Shamus, Payton, and Sin took him into the large office. His parents were taken to another office by Alyssa and Cain. When his father started crying again and his mother too, he knew that Thomas was dead. He sat down hard in the chair and waited. He didn't have to wait long.

"Thomas was found about ten minutes ago. Single bullet to the head and then rolled from a moving vehicle. He was dead before anything happened to him," Sin said in way of starting out. "He was

155

rolled into traffic off of Seventy. Several other vehicles hit him before traffic stopped. They only knew it was him because Verrie Waite called the police station and told them she'd done it and that if they wanted Grace not to suffer the same they were to back the fuck up."

"Where are they now? I'm assuming that we didn't, right?" At Sin's grin, he knew that they hadn't. "I'm not sure I like that look. What the hell have you done?"

"She fucking knows everyone. And if she doesn't, then Alyssa does," Shamus said with a grin. He turned a large whiteboard from the books on the shelves lining the walls and pointed to it. "There are four non marked cars following the limo. Hard to hide one of those suckers. The dead man here was one of drivers, so we called them. They have GPS in all their cars so we have a firsthand look at where they're going."

He knew there was more, so he waited.

"We have a van at every exit between here and wherever. They take turns going to the next exit with a police escort on the back roads. By the time she passes one of them, there are two more racing to the next exit waiting." Shamus handed him a thick file. "This is how we're tracking her."

There were IP, or Internet protocol, addresses for several different devices. They had a complete picture of every place the limo stopped, hesitated, and... Michael looked up. "You think it's necessary to know when she rolls down her window? I mean, this is all good shit, but seriously, we know what radio station she's listening to for Christ's sake."

"It's not to know what she's listening to, it's to hear what is being said. We have a direct line into the thing and can control most of the electronics. We could even shut the sucker off is we wanted." Sin looked at the two men before she continued. "She's still alive. Verrie, or whoever she is, keeps talking to her and Gracie is moaning. I won't let anything happen to her, Michael. None of us will."

"We aren't stopping it just yet because we need her dead to rights." Payton flushed. "I could have said that better. So far, all we have her on is kidnapping and maybe the death of the driver, but nothing else. I don't want her to get off that easily. If she takes Grace somewhere and is prepared, this is all premeditated."

"So you're using my future wife as bait." Michael took a deep breath and tried to reign in his temper. They were playing with his future, his and Grace's.

"No, we're using my sister as the way to end all of this," Sin said softly. "And just so you know, Grace agreed to this."

Chapter 20

Grace hurt. She'd been shot twice now. Verrie had shot her the first time in the arm and Thomas had shot her the next time. She glanced down at her thigh and was glad to see that it had stopped bleeding again. She wasn't sure how much blood a body had in it, but she was reasonably sure her dipstick was nearing the end. A manic giggle escaped her mouth.

The car was still moving. She'd been moving in and out of consciousness since she'd been tossed inside. She'd hit her head on something and wasn't sure what it was until she'd seen the cell phone shattered on the seat next to her. She had cried then, knowing that Michael would be worried if he couldn't get to her.

"Yes. I had to. There was no other way to get them to back off," Verrie said from the front. The next voice, though the same, was slightly different, just enough so that Grace knew that one of the others was speaking to Verrie.

"You had to throw him out of a moving vehicle going eighty miles an hour? Yeah, that didn't draw attention to us."

Grace might have laughed if she wasn't afraid that Verrie or one of the others might hurt her again.

"He shot her again without my permission. What the fuck did you expect me to do? Let him just pop her full of holes before I could get things set up at the house? We have to be as far away as we can before they figure out where she is," Verrie's voice said.

"Yeah. I guess we're not going to get to live in the big house." Grace knew instantly that was her mother. She'd recognize that whiny tone anywhere. "And all that money. Even after we blow them all up at the funeral we can't come back and get it."

Grace tensed. She knew that Thomas was dead. He'd been killed right after he'd shot her. She shuddered when she thought about what he'd been doing to her when she'd awakened. She didn't want to think about what he would have done if she hadn't stopped him before he'd raped her. And what he'd said…he was as insane as her mother.

"You have to let me take you, Grace, before she kills you. It's only fair. You put out for Michael and he's nothing but a bastard. Just let me fuck you this once and then she can kill you and I can tell Michael that I had a piece of you before you died."

She could only stare at him for several seconds. It wasn't until he tried to take her panties off again that she started fighting him. She managed to knee him in the nuts before he hit her with his fist. Then she'd hit him with the heel of her hand in his nose and he'd bled on her. Before she could scramble away from him he'd pulled the gun from the floor and shot her in the leg.

"Now," he'd said. "Lay still until I get you naked. Then you can—"

The car swerved and she fell to the floor. Verrie was screaming at them. Then the loud pop of another gun and Thomas fell atop her, blood everywhere. When Verrie had grabbed him by the hair and ordered her to help her put him in the front seat, she'd done so even when the pain was nearly too much. What Verrie had done with his body made Grace throw up on the floor and the back of the seat.

She'd reached over and opened the passenger door and kicked him out into the street. Grace looked behind them when she heard the squeal of tires and horns blaring just in time to see his body being tossed around from the hood of several cars before he was pulled under a semi. She watched in horror as the truck started to swerve and, finally, it tipped over onto its side. Grace laid her head back on the seat and wept for the way he'd died. No one should have to go like Thomas had. She felt the tears run down her face.

Poor Michael. He didn't deserve this, not his brother being murdered and everything else. She tried to move her leg a little and felt the blood seep from it. When the car stopped, she closed her eyes. She wasn't sure what was going on, but she didn't want Verrie or the others to figure out she was awake.

"Take her inside the house. If she tries to get away, shoot her. And for fuck sake, don't hit her again. There's been a change of plans." Verrie again. "There's a little room in the basement; put her in there and lock the door. She gets away and I'm going to fucking kill you."

"I know what you want me to do," a man's voice said. "Why do you have to treat me like I'm a kid? I got a brain."

Grace wanted to laugh, but didn't. He's got a brain? Then why the fuck wasn't he using it? She moaned before she could stop it and he cuffed her head on the side of the limo. Pain radiated through her body and she saw stars. When she felt the man throw her over his shoulder, she opened her eyes and took a look around.

Nothing, actually less than nothing. No houses, no poles to indicate there was electricity, and the driveway she was being carried up was overgrown with weeds and grass. Just making out the mailbox at the end, it was so faded that she knew that she'd never be able to lead anyone to her even if she could find a way to contact anyone. She wondered how on earth anyone would ever find her when she heard a small voice behind her.

"I can't help you much. I'm holding her from killing you, but you have to be careful. She's…they're draining me." Guinnie patted her on the arm as she walked by and just like that, she was Ginny. "Do we know what we're doing here or are we flying by the seat of our pants? I fucking hate this, Verrie. I thought we had a plan and we were going to stick to it."

"We did until that fucking bastard you befriended decided to have the girl. What the fuck was he thinking shooting her in a moving car? And the fucking idiot nearly shot me when she kicked him in the family jewels. I could care less that he'd shot her; it was the fact that he scared me when he had. Fucking idiot." Verrie faded away as she was lead into a dark stairway.

161

Grace wasn't afraid of the dark; it was the things in the dark that terrified her. She'd been homeless for a while and had spent a lot of her time hiding under awnings and other overhangs. Once, when it was raining really hard, she'd gone to the shelter. When the lights had gone out the crazies had started roaming around. She'd left the place at first light and had never gone back. She felt safer on the streets.

He tossed her on the floor. She supposed that the little cover on the floor was where he was aiming, but he'd missed it enough that she'd banged her head again. Dizziness swamped her and she moaned again. She heard the door close and counted to fifty before she opened her eyes.

The space was small. She was reminded of the coal bin in the building she'd bought. There was a shoot at the rear that had long since been bricked up. She tried to sit up, but she simply didn't have the strength. Crying softly, she pulled out the broken cell phone that she'd managed to put into her pocket before she'd been shot by Thomas.

She thought about all the television shows she'd seen where the phone acted like a GPS thing and someone was always finding the victim with it. She didn't know if it was true or not, but she wasn't going to take any chances. She was terrified of dying and she was going to take every opportunity she could find.

She must have slept. She refused to think that she'd been so weak that she'd slipped away. She nearly screamed when she saw someone sitting in a kitchen chair across from her. She glanced around and didn't see the man, but she didn't know which one she had in front of her either.

"You always were an ungrateful child. Why we had to have you and the others is still a mystery to me. My Roscoe said that you were going to be the most difficult to handle. I suppose he was right."

Her mother. Grace sat up a little and leaned back against the wall before she spoke. This conversation was too long in coming and if she was fucking going to die then she'd have her peace. "You have no right to call me ungrateful. You're the one who fucked us

162

all up. You were so stuck up your husband's ass that you failed to see us for who we were. So, Mother dear, you can fuck the hell off." When Guinevere stood up suddenly and slapped her across the face Grace laughed. "You think that is supposed to make me hurt? Not likely. I washed my hands of you over ten years ago. You're nothing to me."

"You bitch. You should...I should just let her kill you and say fuck the money. But we need it now more than ever. You're going to make it so that we can leave the country and get a new start." Guinevere sat back down in the chair as she continued. "She thought that I could talk some sense into you. Though why she'd think that, I have no idea. You never did do what you were told."

"Say whatever it is you want then get the fuck out. And just so you know, I'll do whatever it takes to see that you spend the rest of your miserable excuse for an existence in a mental institution."

~~~

Joey watched her son. She knew he was hurting, but there was very little she could do about it. She was in pain as well, but it was more a guilty kind of pain than the kind he was going through. Thomas had never been a good son.

She'd tried so hard to like him. She didn't feel guilty for not loving him. That would have been impossible. Thomas hadn't made it easy on anyone after she and Lucas had been married. He resented her and he hated Michael. She'd seen it and was powerless to figure out how to make the stepbrothers get along.

Then when Michael had joined the service it had gotten a little better. With Michael gone and no longer there to remind him of whatever demons he had he actually could go for several days being pleasant. Of course, when he heard anyone mention her son's name he would go into a rage that would scare even his sisters. Even the threat of putting him back in the hospital hadn't worked. He would simply hide for several days, sometimes weeks, before he would show himself again and things would be better. She looked over at Alyssa when she sat beside her.

"When are you due?" she asked the pretty young woman. At her expression Joey thought maybe she'd been keeping her secret

163

close. "I could see the way you looked at dinner. Like you weren't sure if you wanted to toss your cookies over it or cry. I did that a lot with Michael."

"I just found out yesterday. I haven't told anyone yet. We had so much trouble conceiving the first time that I thought for sure I would this time as well." She looked over at her husband. "Cain is going to be so happy. He loves having a big family."

"It was just Michael and I for so long. He was about Trace's age when I married Lucas. We dated for some time before I said yes." She smiled at the memory. "Michael was so happy when I finally said yes. He loves Lucas so much."

"I wouldn't have known they weren't blood if Trace hadn't told me." They both looked over at the little boy who was reading a story to all the children. "He's a wonderful kid. If Grace and Michael weren't already getting married, I might have kept him for myself. Connor just loves him."

Joey watched Trace. She could see the sadness there too. He kept looking up at his father every time the phone rang and she knew he was feeling guilty for not watching Grace. She wanted him to talk to his dad, but he said he'd wait until Grace was home. He said his dad had enough on his mind.

Joey turned to Alyssa. "They'll move here, won't they? Grace and Michael, I mean. He seems to love it here and Trace really enjoys having family too." She felt panicky for reasons she didn't want to think about. Growing old and being alone were scary thoughts. "And I'd forgotten how close Payton and Michael had been. They went to the same college then, when Payton went on to get his police commission, Michael went into the service."

"There's no reason why you can't live here too, or just come to stay as long as you need," Alyssa said softly. "There's plenty of room in this house and there is always the hotels. I can have you and your family a special suite set up so that it's always here for you."

She looked at Alyssa then back at her son. "He's all I have. All I have that is all mine. I love Lucas and his daughters, but…"

Joey looked at her again when she handed her a box of tissues. "I understand. I have…my mother was killed awhile back. My other

164

brother killed her and…well, it was horrible to say the least. I didn't get along with her." She laughed. "Actually, I couldn't stand her. Nathan and I have gotten really close since her death and I'm so happy for that."

Joey had read about it in the paper. Billionaire's Mother Murdered by Brother. And when his trial had ended in a guilty verdict, the entire household had rejoiced. Justice had been served as far as they were concerned. She decided that she really liked Alyssa Waite and the others. She smiled for the first time in days.

"Lucas and I have talked about moving out of the city. And Michael could do his business anywhere. He just needs Internet service, a phone, and an airport." She grinned again at Alyssa. "And having a designer, an author, and a billionaire in the family wouldn't be all that bad either, would it?"

"No, not so much. And we get a great discount on all the clothes and books we want too." Before Joey could comment Payton came into the room. He looked tense.

"The limo stopped about twenty minutes ago. We're going there now. You all should stay here until we can—"

"I'm coming with you. Either you take me or I take you," Michael said as he pulled out his gun. "I don't want to have to hurt you, buddy, but if you don't help me get to Grace I will shoot you in the nuts first."

"Why is it that men always go for the jewels? Do you have any idea how much the woman has to suffer when you do shit like that? Christ, put that thing away before I have to disarm you in front of your kid." Sin tapped her foot until he did it.

Joey was relieved.

"Now, let's play nice or you're going to piss me off and, trust me, you don't want to piss me off today."

Joey burst out laughing and turned to Alyssa again. "And then there is all the free entertainment."

Chapter 21

Michael stared at the house from his cover behind the cruiser. Grace was less than twenty yards from him and he couldn't get to her. He glanced over when Sin slid in to his right side. She glanced at the house before she settled her back against the car.

"Hey. Cain wants to speak to you. Here," she said as she shoved the phone at him. "And just so you know, we all agree with him. But I'm going to help you or I'm beating the shit out of you."

"Has anyone ever told you that you're a tad violent? You should have some anger management classes as soon as this is over." He put the phone to his ear. "Listen, Cain, do you think this could wait? Grace is—"

Cain cut him off. "Go get her. Go into that house and bring out my sister," he said with a hard tone. "You do whatever it takes to get her to us."

Michael looked at Sin again as what Cain was saying sank in. "Cain, she's your mot—"

"No. No, she stopped being anything to any of us the second she started this whole thing. She is a woman who killed and hurt to get what she wanted. You do whatever it takes, do you understand me, Michael? Whatever it takes to bring Gracie back home and this nightmare to end."

"Yes, I understand. But do you? Do you know that Grace is going to be my wife? I have no problem bringing her home, but you're the one who is going to have to live with what you're telling me to do here. Not just today, but for the rest of our lives."

"I've made my peace. My mother is gone as far as I'm concerned. The woman inside there? She's a monster and, what's worse, she's a sick monster." Cain signed heavily. "She hated us all. I can see that now. She hated us so much she stole from us, lied to us, and murdered to get what she thought was hers. Yes, Michael, I can live with this. It's all I've thought of since this started."

Michael wasn't sure what to say to him so he simply closed the connection. He handed it back to Sin and leaned his head back against the car. He looked around the mess that was here.

He could see several media vans parked just beyond the yellow tape some agency had put up. Beyond that there were several dozen cars and vehicles parked along the road all trying to see what was going on. Within shouting distance to him and Sin, there were several vans with letters embossed on the sides, men with the same lettering on flak jackets and vests. There was a tent set up with people milling around a large console and more phones than he'd ever remembered seeing in one of his offices. Michael looked over at Sin when she cleared her throat.

"When I had just joined the Army I met you. I doubt you'd remember. I think they had you pretty doped up on something at the time. You'd been injured, we'd been told, and we weren't to ask you about it. Do you remember being at the base in Texas?"

He'd been hurt a great deal in the years he'd been in the Special Forces. Nothing to the extent that she'd been, but hurt all the same. Shamus had told him that his wife had also been a probable target of the women in the house and he was lucky to have her alive afterwards.

"I'd been held captive for several weeks. I'd been beaten and starved for the better part of that time and, when they weren't doing that, they were trying to get information from me by other means. I just managed to get my ass out when I was mowed down by someone who couldn't read Red Cross on the side of the chopper I was in."

168

Sin grinned at him. "Yeah, seen that a time or two when I was out of country. Not a pretty thing to see one of those monsters go down like that."

He waited for her to say whatever it was she had been leading up to, but she simply grinned again. When she did finally speak he was more confused than before.

"My husband is very smart, did you know that? I don't tell him often enough, but he is." She pulled out her gun, checked the magazine, and then the other clips she had in her belt. He did the same, hoping the two of them weren't going to have a show down. He just wasn't in the mood today. She started talking again as they each shoved their weapons in their holsters.

"Payton said that if she lives she'll be institutionalized. My mother, not Gracie. Drugged up every day and then maybe someone will write an epic story about her life and times. People will copy her and she'll be famous." She grabbed his chin and brought his face to hers. "I want her dead, not famous."

He nodded and stood when she did. He took the vest she handed him and slipped it on as she did the same. When he pulled his Glock out and fit it in his hand he was as ready as he was ever going to be.

"I go lead. You okay with that?"

She nodded.

"The boys aren't going to be happy with us when we come out. You know that, right? They'll be pissy about our messing with their show. Gonna take some fancy talking to keep us out of jail."

"Nah," she laughed. "You're lead asshole, remember? I'm just making sure you don't get dead in the process. You're gonna have to talk yourself out of more than this one if this goes down the way it should." She nodded to a very well-dressed man that had been staring at them for some time. "That's my boss. He'll cover both our asses."

There stood Lieutenant Colonel David Patterson and, before Michael could make any sort of comment, David saluted him. And out of respect for his retired status, Michael returned it. He turned back to Sin with a huge grin. "You do know everybody, don't you?"

169

They turned as one and strode toward the house. Both ignored the shouts and men scrambling behind him. In less than one minute they were on the porch. With a single kick to the door from Michael they were both inside.

A glance around the room showed a couch, chair, and nothing else. When the first person came through the door in front of them, Sin took him out with a single shot to the head. He dropped to the floor without so much as a whimper.

Michael signaled for her to go to the right and he went to the left. Michael walked into what appeared to be the kitchen. Grace was lying on the floor with a woman standing over her with a gun pointed at her.

"Move and she's dead."

Michael nodded once, raised his gun, and fired. He felt a bullet hit him full in the chest seconds before he dropped to his knees. He heard someone shout, but couldn't wrap his mind around the pain and the fact that the woman hadn't shot Grace. He closed his eyes thinking this was a way to go.

~~~

"Do I look like I give a good damn who the fuck you are? And just in case you can't fucking tell, let me explain to you that I don't. Not one fucking bit."

Trace watched the police woman pace as she yelled at the man in the suit. She sure had a potty mouth, Trace thought. And the man she was yelling at seemed to think she was really funny. Grownups were weird. He looked over at his grandma and grandpa while the nurses and doctors ran around the room.

They didn't say much. Trace knew that his uncle Thomas was dead. He'd heard one of the other officers talking about the mess on the highway, but didn't really understand. He almost asked his grandparents, but changed his mind thinking he might not want to know.

The man in the suit sat down next to him on the couch. He sighed really big like his dad did after he got home from work. Trace looked over at him and tried to smile. He was worried and didn't want to talk to anyone right now.

170

"My name is David Patterson. You must be Trace." Trace took his offered hand and shook it. "I understand from your dad's doctor that he's got a couple of busted ribs and his arm is fractured."

Trace sat back and closed his eyes. He hadn't heard that part. He just knew that someone had called the big house and he was put in a car and brought here. The little kids stayed with the nanny. He kind of wished he had, too, until now.

"That's not so bad," he told David. "My mom? Do you know how she is? The man at the desk over there seems to think she's in bad shape. I need for her to be okay so that she and my dad can get married. She isn't going to send me away like my friend's new mom did."

Trace flushed. He hadn't meant to sound so whiny, but the man didn't comment. He'd noticed that around this family. They never made you feel bad or stupid if you said the wrong thing. He liked them all a lot. Trace hoped he got to stay close to them when this was all over.

"Grace is a Waite. She's too mean to do anything but get better."

Trace wasn't sure how to take that. He wasn't sure if the man was insulting his new mom or not so he didn't say anything.

"Mr. Patterson, there's a call for you at the desk. It's Washington, sir. They said it's urgent."

Trace looked up at the man who was dressed in the nicest uniform he'd ever seen.

"There's been a crisis and you're needed."

"There's always a crisis somewhere." David glanced over at him before he spoke to the man again. "Take a message. Then call the President. Tell him that I'm at the hospital with one of my men and that I can't be bothered right now. Tell him I'll call him back when I can."

Trace stared wide-eyed at the man sitting next to him as the man saluted and walked away. "You can do that? I thought you had to do whatever he wanted you to. Wow, you just told the President to take a hike."

Trace flushed again when David laughed. "So I did. He's not so bad, you know. He and I go way back. Your new family, they know him as well. I think your Aunt Alyssa has told him to fu…well, she's told him to take a hike a few times as well."

Trace looked over at his aunt. She was very pretty, but she too could cuss like a sailor, his grandma said. He grinned at her when she winked. To be honest, she was kind of scary too. Not like his Aunt Sin was, but close. He looked over at his new uncles. Two of them were detectives and another was a lawyer. His Uncle Nathan was on a trip in Japan on business and was flying home today, they'd told him. And Uncle Cain was a doctor. He had just about any kind of help if he ever needed it. Grinning, he looked over at David. "I never seen so many people come around for somebody being hurt before. When I broke my arm last year my dad and grandparents were there. Grace sure is loved, isn't she?"

"It's not just Grace, but your dad as well. He impressed them a great deal by barging into that house to get her for them. And the fact that he got hurt doing it makes them love him all the more." David nodded toward the people sitting on the couch next to the rest of them. "There are the Grants. Couldn't ask for a better group of people either. You're getting yourself a good family, son. They'll do right by you."

He certainly hoped so. He wanted them to like him. He was afraid they'd want them all to go back to New York and not return. This was scary stuff. Thomas had been a bad man for a long time, almost as long as Trace had remembered. He was always drunk or high too.

There were things he knew they tried to hide from him. The fact that Thomas was a drunk was one of them. He was also mean to some of the people who worked for his grandparents. He didn't know why he was, but Uncle Thomas seemed to have enjoyed being mean, like it was his job or something. Trace bowed his head. He shouldn't be talking about him like this, he realized. He was dead, after all.

Trace looked up when David stood up. The doctor was coming toward him and right behind him was a wheelchair with his dad in

172

it. Trace tried not to cry, but seeing his father, even as bad as he looked, was the best thing he'd ever seen. Rushing toward him, he started to hug him when he stopped suddenly. His dad pulled him close and wrapped his good arm around him.

"Christ, I missed you," his dad said and Trace started crying. He didn't realize how scared he'd been until that minute. Holding him and being held by him was the greatest feeling.

"Mom is still in surgery. The doctor said that she had been beaten up pretty bad. They won't tell me anything 'cause I'm just a kid." Trace wiped at the tears and moved back so that everyone else could get a hug.

"Let me see what I can find out," Cain said. "I've been up to check twice now and all they've been able to tell me is that she's still in surgery." He walked away and to the desk.

"Calling her Mom now, are you? You're moving faster than me."

Trace laughed at his dad.

"Next thing you know, you and she will be eloping and I'll be left holding the bag."

"Then you'd better get your game on, old man. I need a mom and you're slacking." Trace laughed when his dad cuffed him lightly on the chin. "She said it was okay. Should I have asked you first?"

"Absolutely not. You and she are going to have to work on your own relationship. I'll just try real hard not to piss her off too much." His dad was moved over to the couch where he'd been sitting. "You still okay with her and I marrying?"

Trace nodded, then leaned in to whisper to him. "I told you I'd protect her and I didn't. I told...if I had gone to the airport with her instead of staying at the house with her family then—"

"Then you'd be hurt too. Don't think like that. You did what needed to be done. That woman would have had you both and I would have been insane without knowing. Well, insaner anyway. I need you as much as I do Grace, son."

They sat for another two hours before they got to see Grace. Cain had told them that she was in recovery and would be for a bit.

She came through surgery like a trooper and they didn't foresee any problems with her injuries. Trace laid down on the couch and fell asleep. He'd had a really long day.

Chapter 22

Michael tried to get comfortable in the chair, but his ribs hurt and his arm was aching again. He looked longingly at the bed Grace was sleeping in. What he wouldn't give to crawl in it beside her and sleep for the next hundred years. Smiling, he wondered if that would be long enough.

"Come over here," she whispered to him. "I want to feel you close to me. If you don't hog all the covers I think we can just manage it."

"I was thinking the same thing. I want to just stretch out beside you for a little while." He glanced over at his mother on the fold-out couch. "She wouldn't leave. She said she needed to be here in case you needed her."

"I need you both. Please? Just until they make you leave."

He moved toward the bed, toeing off his shoes.

They needed to talk, he knew that. Things had happened in that house and the police, along with several agencies, had been trying to get him to come to their respective offices for the last few hours. He'd gone to Patterson to see if he could get them to back off and he'd not heard a single word from them since. He pulled the covers back and gently laid beside her. She turned around and laid her head on his chest, careful of his cast.

"How are you feeling?" he asked her after a minute or two. "The doctor said you'd be okay to go home in a few days. But

175

you'll have to take it easy. And stay off your leg for a bit." He'd told him a great deal more, but he didn't want to share that with her right now. He was happy she was alive.

He felt her laugh. "Cain came in and told me what the doctor said. You can't give me half-truths when I have a doctor at my beck and call."

"Your brother and I are going to have to lay down some ground rules where you're concerned," he told her with a pouty tone. "You lost a great deal of blood, but they gave you some to replace it. He said that the bullet wound in your leg is going to be your biggest concern. He said that there is some deep muscle damage and that you'll need physical therapy for a long time. By the way, Sin said she'd run with you in the mornings if you want."

She nodded before speaking. "She said you and her have been to the range and that she outshot you nearly every time."

"She and I shot three clips and she hit the target once more than me," he huffed. "You know that she has a gun on her all the time? I'm betting that she's in her daughter's room right now reading her the *Three Little Pigs* with a Glock strapped to her ankle. She is one scary woman."

She laughed like he hoped she would. Then she was quiet for so long he thought she'd fallen asleep. When she started talking he didn't interrupt her, but let her say whatever she wanted.

"They wanted me dead at first. They said that as soon as I was dead my 'mother' would have a nervous breakdown and that she'd be unable to attend my funeral. There was going to be a bomb in the casket with me and it was going to take everyone out." He felt a tear hit his chest. "They were going to kill the children as well so that they could inherit all of the money."

Michael had figured it had to do with the money. He'd been told by all of them that Roscoe had gone so far as to kidnap one of his own daughters and hold her at gun point to get what he wanted. It seemed that Guinevere had wanted the same thing.

"Guinnie was trying to help me escape when Verrie came back. The house...I was getting out of the house when she hit me with the door. I was trying to get out and get back to you, but she hit me with… Oh, Michael, the things she said she'd done, the things she said she was going to do."

And that was what the police wanted to talk to her about. They'd been to the empty apartment building that Guinevere had been staying at. So far they'd found four bodies. They'd been mutilated almost beyond knowing what sex they were. It seemed that at least one of the women had an MO that was going to make it easy to close a great many cases.

"They won't tell me what happened, only that you and Sin came into the house like some sort of avenging angels and saved the day." She shifted so that her hand was on his chest and her chin resting on it. "Did you and Sin come in with your weapons drawn, ready to be my saviors?"

He leaned up and kissed her briefly on the mouth. When she moaned he cupped the back of her head and brought her to his mouth again. He decided she was the best sort of drug and found he didn't want to stop kissing her. She pulled back only because the door opened.

"I'm sorry, Miss Waite, but we really need to get some questions answered. Your lawyer is right outside and he said that if you want him here he is ready, and if you didn't then, as your brother, he was coming in. Either way, he was ready." The agent looked back at the door before he spoke again. "You have a very protective family. That big man said if I made you upset he was going to castrate me and make me…well, as a doctor I thought it was his duty to help people, not harm them."

Michael laughed and started to get up, but Grace tightening her body to his had him staying. He glanced over at his mom when he heard her stirring. He wasn't sure what she wanted to know or not so he gently said her name until she woke.

"Oh my, I'm so sorry. I've been…oh, the police." His mother looked over at them before speaking. "I need to know. I know I have no right to ask you, but…well, Thomas was my stepson and I want to know if he…did he…" Michael got up then and went to her. "He didn't hurt her, did he?" she asked him softly.

"I don't think so. I'll find out and let you know. Why don't you—"

"He didn't. He wasn't helping me, but he didn't hurt me. I think they might have promised him things that he thought...I don't believe it was necessary what they did to him, but if it's any comfort at all he was gone before he was thrown from the car."

Michael looked at Grace as she spoke to his mom. He didn't know how, but he absolutely knew she was lying. And he loved her all the more because of it.

Joey moved to the bed and hugged Grace. They were both crying when his mom left, and it took a few minutes for Grace to get herself back under control. Michael doubted that very many things bothered her and knowing that her feelings for his mom were this deep made him feel very good.

The agent, Jeffery Roy Weber, and he did use his full name, asked if he could sit down. "It's been a real long day. I doubt that I sat down for more'n five minutes all day."

He stretched out his legs and made a production of getting settled. Michael had used the same "good old boy" routine many times before. Both in business and in the service. He was about to point out that he could cut the crap, but Grace beat him to it.

"Agent Weber, let's call an apple and apple here and cut to the chase. I'm a New Yorker. Not born and bred, mind you, but pretty close. So how about you ask what you want and I'll answer to the best of my knowledge." She looked over at him. "In case it escaped your notice, this man and I were into some serious necking when you walked in and I, for one, would like to get back to it."

Michael looked at the agent's face and thought maybe if there was a more shocked-looking face in the world he had to see it. The agent looked over at him like he wanted to say something. But Michael agreed with Grace. They had more important things to do than to answer questions.

"I agree with her. Ask or don't, but make it quick or you might get a few things known to you that you might not have bargained for." The man blustered for several seconds. "You're eating at your time, sir. Get to it."

~~~

The next morning, they had her sitting in a chair and Grace started feeling sorry for herself. She was black and blue over most of her body. Her forehead had fifteen stitches and both her eyes were blackened. She could get around slowly with the help of a walker, but it hurt like hell and she couldn't remember the last time she'd washed her hair, much less her entire body. When the door to her room opened she nearly snarled at the person to go the fuck away.

"You know you look like you want to shoot someone," Sin said in way of greeting. "I'm armed if you want to make someone here a good target. There's that little shit in the lobby that I wouldn't mind making skip a few times."

Making a person skip had been something that the two of them said about shooting someone. She had said she didn't want to kill everyone that pissed her off, but she would like to make them dance a bit by shooting at their feet. Sin had told her that would be more like skipping than dancing and it had stuck.

Grace burst into tears as her other sisters came into the room. They each took a seat and sat on the bed as well. Grace took the tissue that Alyssa handed her and none of them said a word until she'd blown her nose twice more.

"You must think I'm a ninny. I've been through all this crap over the past few days and here I am upset because I have a few bruises on my face." She looked at all of them before she said what she really thought. "I should have told you all. It's...this is totally my fault that all of this happened to you—"

"That's enough. You had nothing to do with the insanity of one person. My God, you were hurt just as much as any one of us," Jazzie snapped. "Had you told us then, I'm sure that the same things would have happened. We were all duped by her."

Grace didn't believe that for a minute, but she didn't say anything. It was hard enough trying to get a grip on what had transpired in that house without adding the burden of trying to explain why she felt the way she did.

179

"Spill it," Sin told her quietly. "If you don't then your head will explode and poor Michael will be all alone. By the way, I kinda like him. He's an ass most of the time, but I can take him down a peg or two on the range quick enough when he gets out of hand."

Grace knew that she had to tell them. She looked to the door when the others walked in. She smiled at Cain and the other men in her family now. Most of them she didn't know very well, but she did know that they loved their spouses with all of their hearts.

"Mother wasn't always evil like she was toward us. There was a side of her, Guinnie; that was the kindness in her that the others couldn't...no, that's not right, the others wouldn't show. Even Mother couldn't be what Guinnie was."

"The child, Guinnie was the child, right?"

Grace nodded at Quinn's question.

"I met her then. I was really sick. I think I was about ten and Mother came into my room. I had the feeling that Mother was there and when she began to speak I realized she wasn't acting the same. Like her voice was even different."

"They all had very distinct mannerisms and voices. Even their dress was different." Grace smiled at the women who were dressed so differently that it was amazing. Alyssa was dressed in torn jeans and a sloppy t-shirt, tennis shoes with no socks. Quinn had on dress pants, a tailored blouse, and heels. Then there was Jazzie who, even in her glowing maternal state, looked as if a cockatoo had been the color idea for her clothes. Sin was dressed as one would think of a woman who'd spent the last ten years of her life in the armed services—cargo pants, black t-shirt, and boots. Grace was willing to bet that she had a gun somewhere on her person, more than likely two of them. Sin's twin Lilliane was dress in a denim dress with sandals, and a huge purse.

"Tell us what happened at the house. I know you spoke to the police already and they cleared you. Tell us what happened after you left the house." Michael came to sit beside her as Lilliane asked her. He took her hand as she began.

"Thomas tried to...he wanted me. He said that I was going to die anyway and that Verrie had promised that he could have me. I

180

was in the backseat with him when he tried to rape me." She looked at Michael before she continued. "Verrie was driving and she told him to wait. But he wouldn't. He told her that he wanted his payment now. I don't know what she owed him for, but he was collecting."

"Thomas had been trouble all his life. His problem was that his mother hadn't made him do anything he didn't want and when he did something that got him into trouble she simply paid off whoever he had injured." Michael looked around the room before looking back at her. "He hated me. I never understood why until the funeral. His friends…well, the ones that had been his mother's acquaintances, had told me that they could never understand why she let him get by with so much. And that his hatred toward me was because my mother had always been so good to me."

"So he was jealous," Payton said. "I knew that little shit. Sorry, but he was. And the longer I was around him, the more I wanted to kick is fucking ass. There wasn't a kid around that had it so easy yet seemed to think it wasn't enough."

"I'm not sure. I only met him the one time and that was at the birthday dinner for Trace." Grace flushed a little. "He made a pass at me then. I didn't know how to react. It was as if he thought I was…well, it matters little now. But back to the house. I was in and out of it by then. There was this man and he lifted me out of the limo. I'm not sure what his relationship was to the others, but he did everything they told him to. He also seemed to understand that they were four separate people, yet he only listened to Verrie."

"His name was Bob Smith, if you can believe it," Shamus told them as he opened a folder. "He took care of your mother off and on over the years. He was her keeper, I guess. Especially when your father spent time behind bars, he'd hire him to make sure she didn't get into trouble. Or too much trouble, it seemed. She was in a great deal of it by the time she made it back here."

"That explains a lot. When we got to the house, every time she would become another he would simply start calling her by that name. At one point they had an argument with him and he fought with each of them as if they were three separate beings." Grace

181

remembered how surreal that had been. "There were times when I would swear that he was more their father than anything else."

"So he took you into the house, then what?" Cain asked. Grace felt sorry for him the most. He'd been the protector of them all for so long. To have this happen and it be out of his control was probably eating away at him.

"I was taken to the basement and put on the floor. The room was small, but they'd been prepared for me. The plastic on the floor had been the first clue that they planned to actually kill me, but I think something went wrong. Verrie said that they had to keep me or they wouldn't get anything."

"They ransomed you," Alyssa said. "We got a call just after Thomas was killed and she said that she wanted ten million dollars and they'd give you back. We think it was because of the police being on them so quickly."

"Thanks to you." Nathan handed Grace the broken phone as he walked over and kissed Jazzie. "You turned it on and activated the GPS. That was a great way to find you and, even broken like it was, it still let us pinpoint you within a few yards. Do we even want to know how it got broken?"

She held it in her hand and looked at Michael. "I was trying to call you. I was sure you could hear me and I actually thought of you finding me that way, but Guinnie told me to run. I forgot it in the car when I took off. After I was shot the first time I also managed to drop my gun."

"I told you she had the bead on her," Sin said with a laugh. "Didn't I tell you my Gracie would get the jump on her and wouldn't let me down?" She laughed again as she high-fived her husband.

"Yes, you did. Now sit down and be quiet before I have to paddle your bottom. Go on, Grace," Payton told her. "Tell us what happened next and miss know-it-all will hush."

Grace burst out laughing. Then she looked around the room again. These people were her family. All of them held her safe when she needed it, and even when she didn't think she did.

"I love you guys. All of you so very much." She wiped at the tears on her cheeks. "You've no idea how much I wished I could have come home, but...I should have known you'd be there for me."

"Well of course we would. You're our family, aren't you?" Alyssa looked at her, then around the room. "Now let's finish this up so that we can get this show on the road and get you home tomorrow. And I, for one, would like to know when the wedding is."

Grace was afraid to look at Michael. She was sure he was going to change his mind about them. Before she could come up with any kind of answer, he answered. But not the way she'd thought.

"If we can hold off until she's committed then I think we can do it anytime you can get it together. But not too long. I want to be able to claim her before we start a family."

Grace started to ask him what he meant when she suddenly got what he'd said. "Committed? Who? Mother?"

Kathi S. Barton

Chapter 23

Guinevere tried to talk to any of the others, but it was entirely too much effort. She wanted to ask them what had happened, when they were going to get their money, and what the fuck they thought they were doing shutting her out. She had to force her eyes open, but it, too, was a chore.

"It's time for your medications, Mrs. Waite. Come on now, you know they won't let you go out into the world without some nice happy juice."

Guinevere looked up at her with half-closed eyes.

"Come on now. It's time to get up and get ready."

"Ready," was all she could manage. What the hell, *ready*? All she could think to do was sleep. She certainly didn't want to go anywhere.

"Yes. Come on. The courts won't wait all day for you. If you can put your good arm around me, I'll lift you to the chair."

"Verrie. Where?" She needed someone there to tell her what the hell was going on. She couldn't function without at least one of them to help her.

Suddenly she was out of the bed and into a sitting position. There was nothing for her to do but let the person put the handcuffs on her arms and attach her to the chair. She tried to think, tried her very best to bring someone to her, but nothing. Then there was the small burn of something on her arm.

185

"There you go. Nice and calm now. As soon as I get you wrapped up in the blankie, I'll get you going. There's a good girl."

"Verrie," she tried again. "Where…where am I? Where are the…where are the others?"

"You can't see anyone just yet. Not until the trial is over at any rate. Then if I don't miss my guess, and I've never been wrong about one of these, you'll be spending the rest of your life in the State House for the Criminally Insane."

Guinevere looked at the man standing in the door way.

"After that, well, it's anyone's guess."

"Who?" Guinevere asked. She felt the stirring of one of the others, but they didn't speak to her. She had a small memory from one of the others, but there wasn't enough of a connection to help her figure out any more than he was a man who Verrie wanted to fuck.

"I told you before, Miss Waite, when we're here there is no need for you to pretend. And if you do it again I will have someone else come and talk to you." He sat on the bed as he pulled out files and spoke to her. "The trial is set for two hours from now. Once we get into the courtroom they'll take you to your seat. Now, as I've said before, you can't cause any sort of ruckus or the judge won't let you speak on your behalf."

She sat up a little straighter in her wheelchair and looked down at her body. She had on a pair of jogging pants that were bright orange and her shirt, one that had something printed on the front that she simply couldn't make out, was just as orange. Her socks, also an orange that was more suited to pumpkins than clothing, were barely on her feet. They sort of reminded her of her husb—

"Jail? I'm in jail? No. That can't be right. There's been a mistake." She felt another stir of one of the others, but again, not enough to tell which one. "There's something wrong."

The man sitting across from her glared for several minutes. Guinevere might have been uncomfortable by his stare if she wasn't still trying to wrap her mind around the fact that she was in jail.

"Miss Waite, for the tenth time, you are not in jail. This is merely a holding place for you until the judge makes the decision as to what sort of facility you will go to. Then when the time is right, you'll be taken before the court to determine if you are able to stand trial and if you are sane enough to be tried on the crimes against you."

"What crimes?" she asked him. "I didn't do anything wrong. It was all that money-grubbing whore's fault. She's the one who killed my Roscoe."

"Yes, that's it. Keep up that sort of talk and you'll be spending the next fifty years of your life in a place just like this one, only the state tends to be little less friendly when they're footing the bill."

The laughter in her mind made her skin crawl. She hadn't been prepared for it to sound so chilling. And when Guinnie spoke, Guinevere felt her blood run just a little colder.

"You should have listened to me. Had you or any of the others just given me my due then I wouldn't have had to resort to such extreme measures. Especially in light of what has happened to you."

Guinevere waited for Guinnie to continue. When she didn't, she asked her what she meant. What had she done?

"Done? Why, I did what you should have done many, many years ago. I ended this. I wish his aim would have been just a little better, but... Well, how do you like our new home? Not fancy, but we're safe."

"What have you done? Tell Verrie I need to speak to her this minute. I want to speak to Verrie or Ginny right this fucking minute." Guinevere looked at the man as he stood. She hadn't realized she'd spoken out loud until that moment. The laughter made her think that Guinnie knew much more than she was letting on.

"Miss Waite, this is not the least bit funny. If it weren't for the fact that I know you can't move then I would leave here and never return." He moved his chair back from her a few feet before he began to speak again. "Now, the trial is set for today. Then when the findings find you—"

"You should know that his aim killed Ginny. She was in the front when he fired. Too bad that he only managed to put the bullet

187

into your frontal lobe and not all the way through your sick mind." Guinevere ignored the man for the child in her mind. *"And poor Verrie. She went off the deep end...well, deeper end just after they tied us down after surgery. I swear, there are times when I can still hear her scream."*

Guinevere tried to shake her head to clear it. When she did speak again it was only in her mind and not so the lawyer, Peter March, she remembered his name, could hear her. It upset him for some reason.

"Who's aim? You are to tell me what happened and right now, Guinnie. I demand that you share what you know." Guinevere knew she was in no place to demand anything and, apparently, so did Guinnie.

"Demand? I don't think so. Since your...accident, things have been going very nicely. But as I choose to tell you what happened, I will. Michael, my Gracie's soon-to-be husband, shot you in the head. I had hoped that I could have controlled Ginny just a bit longer, but she took over at the last second and jerked from the bullet. As it is now, you've had some extensive brain surgery. Just enough to get rid of Verrie and, of course, Ginny. Now, my dear, it's just the two of us. And I'm not going to leave you until you do what is necessary."

"Necessary? I don't..." Guinevere stiffened. *"You can't mean for me to kill myself? Why what would my children... No, I won't do it. Not now, not ever. And if you think you can drive me to it then—"*

"Oh, I don't think I can, Guinevere dear, I will do just that. And starting today. You're either going to give me the peace that I want or I never give you any again."

Guinevere was suddenly afraid. *"I'll just escape. I'll just walk out one day and—"*

The chilling laughter again and then Guinnie spoke. *"Walk? I'm sorry. Did I forget to mention that you are also paralyzed?"* She laughed again. *"Michael is now my favorite person. And before you think you can talk any of your children into taking care of you I've already spoken to Grace. She is going to make sure that none of them ever come to see you again."*

188

Guinevere looked at Peter again. He was staring at her. She had no idea what he'd been saying and, for the life of her, she couldn't drudge up enough concern to wonder if what he'd been saying was of any importance. She simply stared.

By the time that he left her she had not only discovered that she couldn't move her feet, but she couldn't even twitch her fingers. She tried to will her body to move, to do anything, but all she could do was hear Guinnie.

"Now, let us begin. I read somewhere that reading is good for the mind. And there was a time when I read a book to Grace. She loved the story so much that I read it to her nightly. Today and everyday for the rest of our lives, I'm going to read the same story to you."

Guinevere was almost afraid to ask. *"What story do you think you're going to read to me?"*

"Green Eggs and Ham, of course." *Guinevere could hear her laughter again.* "'I am Sam. I am Sam. Sam I am. That Sam I am. That Sam I am. I do not like that Sam I am…'"

~~~

Grace had been home a week when she got the call from the hospital. Her mother had committed suicide. It hadn't been something she was surprised about, but the timing. She would have thought that Guinnie would have taken a lot longer to drive her mother to it. She hung up the phone and sat in the chair in the kitchen, feeling nothing. She told Cain when he came in to get a glass of tea.

"You said she would do it. I just…I'm not even sure I care. How about you?"

She shook her head at his question.

"I'll call the rest of them later. Oh, there's a letter for you from some lawyer. I laid it on the table. I didn't know you were in here."

Grace went to the dining room table and picked up the light gray envelope. It had the return address of New York. She almost threw it away, but opened it instead. It was from Matthew Gray, a name she barely remembered.

189

It said she was to come to his office in the morning. There would be a plane for her and a ride to and from the airport. She felt the tears roll down her face as she read the reasons why. She was to finalize the sale of the Washington building and other matters.

Michael's lawyer had finally contacted her. She'd been expecting it for over a week now. After he'd left her the day after she'd talked to the FBI. She hadn't been able to give him back his ring and wondered if and when he'd realize that he'd didn't have it. Now, it seemed, he was going to get it all.

She'd told him she couldn't marry him. He didn't say much at first, but the more she told him, the angrier he got until later, she'd told him why.

"I could be just like her. The doctor and even Cain said it could happen. Plus, the papers are already making it sound as if you're marrying some lunatic and I know your business deals have slowed." She tossed him the paper open to the financial page. "Your stock has dropped over eighteen points since this all hit the paper."

He didn't even bother looking at it as he threw it in the trash can. "So? You think I care what one paper says about you and me? I don't. I love you." He started to come toward her and she raised her hand to stop him. "You're really going to tell me that all this matters to you?"

"It should matter to you as well. You have a reputation to uphold." She turned her back to him as she continued. "You should go. I can't...I won't marry you. You should simply move on with your life."

The door closing to the room felt like a shot to her heart. He had to leave. The papers were crucifying him daily and she knew that it would only get worse as the trial started. She sat down hard on the chair and looked out over the parking lot. It was dark by the time she realized how much pain she was in and that she'd not given him back his ring.

She made arrangements to be at the Cunningham building the next afternoon. She didn't want to go. It was hard enough knowing that she'd have to face him and just wanted it to be over with. Grace tried on five different outfits, none of which fit her well. She'd been losing weight and it was beginning to show. She finally had to borrow one from Lilliane and smiled when she realized it was one of hers.

That was another thing that had suffered. Her designs had simply stopped. She'd not made a single thing, even to think up a design, since this whole thing had happened. Her staff had been working on putting together the orders that were being generated by the new catalogue and she wondered if, after this one, there'd be a Gracie Anne catalogue.

"Good morning, Miss Waite. If you'll please follow me I'll take you to see Mr. Gray."

Grace followed the pretty little secretary, wondering where Mr. Gray's wife had gone.

"Would you like anything while you're waiting?"

"No, thank you," she told the woman as she left the room. Grace tried to sit and, when that didn't work, she paced. By the time Matt came into the room she was a ball of nervous energy.

"Hello, Grace. You look like shit, if you don't mind my saying so."

She nearly started to cry, but clenched her fist and said nothing.

"Michael doesn't look any better, in case you're wondering."

"I wasn't, but thanks. What is it you need from me, Mr. Gray? I thought all the papers were signed when the deal was closed." She sat down again when he did. "I tried to tell you several days ago that I don't want anything from Mr. Cunningham and now—"

"I'm not representing Michael. I called you in here because of another client. Michael doesn't even know you're here." She looked at the door when it opened and she stood. "Trace, have a seat."

She looked at Matt then back at Trace. "I don't know what's going on. Why am I here if this has nothing to do with the Washington building?"

"I wanted to talk to you. Uncle Matt said I could get you here like this so I paid him to be my lawyer." He looked at her with sad eyes. "You didn't say goodbye. Are you mad at me because I didn't protect you?"

Grace felt all the wind rush out of her body. She'd never thought of how this would affect him. She glanced over at Matt then back at Trace before she began. "No. If you had come with me then you would have gotten hurt. The reasons they took me had nothing at all to do with you and I wanted you to be safe."

"Dad says that you hate him. That nobody could love somebody like you said you did and just let them walk away." Trace looked at the door before he continued in a lower voice. "He's been mean since you left. I don't want to be with him anymore."

Grace stood. "Did he hurt you, Trace?" He nodded and she turned to Matt. "Where is he?"

Matt stood too. "You don't need to see him. This is between you and Trace and—"

"He's in his office," Trace said quickly. "He's talking to…well, he's probably yelling at my grandma again. He yells at everyone and he's…he's sending me to school next week."

That pissed her off. She was out the door and striding to his office before she knew it. Not even bothering to knock, she walked into his office and threw back the door. He stood up just as she came around the side of his desk.

"What the fuck do you think you're doing sending him away? I'll have you know what's going on between us has nothing to do with him. You send him to a military school and I'll…I'll come here and punch you right in the balls." He simply stared at her so she went on. "And if I hear that you've been mistreating your mother I'll send my sister after you. She has it out for you already. The nerve of you telling her boss that you beat her on the—"

His mouth covered hers. His warmth and strength filled her. And as his arms encircled her she leaned into him. A soft moan escaped her mouth as she wound her fingers into his hair. When she felt the wall behind her she pulled back slightly to try and regain control of the conversation.

"No," Michael breathed against her neck. "Not yet. I haven't had enough of you yet. Not nearly enough."

His hands seemed to be everywhere, cupping her breast and tugging at her nipple. He pulled her leg over his hip and lifted her higher. When she was ready to beg him to take her he suddenly stopped and stiffened. Before she could help it a whimper spilled from her mouth.

"Michael, do put the woman down. I do not want to watch you make love to her when we're in the middle of an important conference call."

Grace peeked over Michael's shoulder at his mother.

"Hello, dear. Your timing could have been a little better, but come and sit down while we finish this deal. Are you still there, Arnold?"

Laughter greeted her query. "Yes. And what I wouldn't give to be where you are right now. Christ, the stodgy Michael Cunningham forgetting business for a woman. She must be one hell of beauty to stop him in his tracks."

"She is. Quite smart too if she finally shows up here to tell him she loves him and can't live without him," Joey said. "Do you, Grace? Do you love my little boy enough to come back here and forgive him? He's been—"

"Mother, that's enough. Arnold, if we could finish this up tomo—"

"What do you mean forgive him? Forgive him for what?" Grace looked from Joey to Michael. "Forgive you for what?"

"I shot your mother. It's the real reason you sent me packing, isn't it? I never thought of it at the time, but after I got home and read about it in the paper it occurred to me that you were mad at me because I'd shot your mother." He pulled back from her, but didn't turn around. She glanced down and saw that he was hard, straining against the fly of his pants. She looked back up at his face when he groaned. It took her several seconds to realize what he'd said.

"I don't hate you for shooting my mother. Hell, I wish I could have done it myself. Where did you get a stupid idea like that?" She looked at the door as it opened to reveal Trace and Matt. "You did this."

Michael turned then to look at the two of them. Matt flushed and Trace looked at anything but his dad. When Michael finally spoke she wanted to brain him all over again.

193

"You're grounded, young man. And you." He pointed at Matt. "You're fired. What the fuck were you two thinking anyway?"

"Maybe we were hoping she'd come up here and light into you so that you could have some make-up sex and realize that you love her." Trace's face bloomed to a shade of red that Grace knew was burning. "I love her too, you know."

Chapter 24

Michael stared at his son. He reached for Grace's hand and held it as he moved back to his chair. His own son had done what he'd not been able to. He'd gotten her here. Pulling her into his lap, he was glad when she didn't fight him.

"If you all will excuse us, I think Grace and I have something to say to each other. And please have my calls held until tomorrow. Arnold." The man answered and Michael grinned. "If we could take this up tomorrow, then I'm sure we can come to a mutual understanding."

"Sure thing, buddy. Just don't make it too early. I have a feeling my wife is going to be plenty happy to hear about this when you call."

They all left his office and he sat still. He held Grace in his arms and felt the world settle around him. He was at peace for the first time since he'd pulled the trigger. Her speaking made him hold her tighter.

"She died today. Well, she killed herself."

He didn't need to ask who. He knew it was her mother.

"Guinnie told me that she'd drive her over the edge and I guess she succeeded."

"How did it happen, honey? No one else was hurt, were they? I mean, she didn't try to hurt anyone and they had to shoot her?" Christ, he hoped no one else had been hurt by this woman.

195

"She choked herself to death by eating a book. I didn't even know she liked to read, but they said she'd asked for a few books she'd read to us as a child." She pulled back to look at him. "Doctor Seuss books, as a matter of fact. Mother had never read to us before, Guinnie had."

He pulled her back into his arms. "I love you, Grace. More than ever, I love you. Please tell me that you love me too."

She was quiet for a few minutes. She pulled back this time and looked up at him before she leaned in and kissed him. The touch of her mouth against his was soft and hungry at the same time, warm and sensual too. When she slid her tongue along the seam of his mouth, he opened under her gentle assault.

Turning her in his lap, she straddled him. Cupping her ass, he pulled her to his cock and moaned when she arched her back, seemingly offering him her breast. Taking one of them into his mouth Michael nipped hard and ran his hands up and under the short skirt of the dress she had on. Encountering her warm, bare flesh nearly had him tossing her onto the desk and taking her. Instead, he lifted her as he stood. Striding toward the conference table, he laid her over it as he stepped back.

"I need to be inside of you now. Then I want to take you home with me and make love to you—fuck." He rubbed his hands up her thighs as he remembered he didn't have a house anymore.

"Michael? What is it?" She sat up and stared at him through her hooded eyes. "Do you want me to go home?"

"No. Christ, no. I don't have a house. I sold it. Well, Trace and I sold it. And it's too far to take you to the one I just bought." He tried to think, but she kept distracting him. "Baby, you keep that up and I won't be able to think at all."

She opened her legs wider then ran her foot up his cock. Back and forth she went until he had to lean on the table and hold on. She was slowly killing him. When she pulled the small top up and over her breast, Michael's cock jumped.

"Grace," he moaned. "You're going to make me come if you keep this up. And I'm not sure how long I'm going to last once I get you naked anyway."

196

"Where's your house, Michael? Why is it so far away?" Her voice was a purr and he felt it as it moved over him like a touch. "I suddenly find myself in need of your big bed."

"I was coming…Christ, Grace, that fucking feels good." Her toes caressed him and he had to take several breaths before he could continue. "I was coming to Ohio to live there with Trace. We were going to wear you down until you took us back. Take off your panties for me."

He moaned when she reached down, pulled her dress to her hips and over them, and ran her fingers over the top of her mound. She was soaking wet. He could almost taste her honey and her scent was making him wild with need.

Dropping to his knees, he buried his nose in her heat. She moaned when he pulled her closer to the edge of the table. He had to have a taste. And he wasn't stopping until he had his fill.

"Marry me, Michael. Please?"

He looked up at her as she leaned up on her elbows to watch him.

"Marry me and give me children. Marry me so that I can be Trace's mother. Please?"

He stood up and pulled her to him. "We're going to find the closest hotel I can find then I'm going to finish what we started."

He was out of the building dragging her behind him when he realized he didn't have a coat and no wallet. He turned to stare down at her.

"I'm staying at the one just over there. If we hurry, we can cross the street now and be in my room before anyone knows you're gone."

Michael grinned at her suggestion. He picked her up and tossed her over his shoulder. He was nearly across the street when the light changed, but no one beeped at them. When a cabbie opened his door and stepped out of his taxi Michael wasn't sure what to expect, but his clapping wasn't anywhere near what he had anticipated. Then one by one everyone got out and started clapping until the first man started laughing.

"Can't hold traffic up forever young man. Take the pretty lady inside and make her happy."

Michael laughed. "Yes, sir," he told him, and walked the rest of the way to the sidewalk. When he got there he dropped her back onto her feet and much to the happiness of everyone watching, he kissed her. "Grace, my dear, I accept." He picked her up again and walked to the door. "But we need to do this soon. I want to help you model the next catalogue coming up and I want you large with my baby."

~~~

Michael took her into his arms when they reached the elevator. He was so hungry for her that he nearly took her on the floor. If the door hadn't opened when it did, he wasn't sure he might not have. She lead him down the hall and every few steps he would pull her back to him and taste another part of her; breasts, neck, ears, it didn't matter. He had her now and he wasn't letting her go. By the time they had her door opened and inside he had his belt undone and she had managed to get his top three buttons unbuttoned.

"Hurry," she told him as she moved against him. "Michael, I need for you to take me. Please, you have to hurry."

It was as if a peace came over him. He gentled his hands and held her to him. He was going to savor her, savor what they were about to do. This woman meant the world to him and he wanted her to know it right now. Pulling her from him, he looked down at her face. "I'm going to make love to you. Slowly. And I'm going to go at my pace. I want to make love to you to show you that I love you. Will you let me?" He knew that if she begged him again he'd be done, but she only nodded her head. "Go to the side of the bed. I want to undress you."

She nodded again and did as he asked. He could see the pulse pounding at her throat. He could feel her breath on his face. She even smelled good, sexual need and her own special scent that nearly sent him over the edge. He ran his fingers down her arm and smiled when she shuddered.

"Michael, please don't tease me. Please, make love to me."

He looked at her face as he touched her. He grinned when she whimpered again. "Do you really want to have children? I spoke to Trace about it. He's very excited about having younger siblings." She moaned when he cupped her breast through her dress. "He seems to think you have the coolest family ever."

"He's been calling Cain and Alyssa. He even called—oh, Michael, please." He leaned down and took her hard nipple into his mouth. She swallowed twice before she spoke again. "Sin, he called Sin to ask her where the best schools were."

Dropping to his knees, he moved his hands up and down her thighs. She put her hand on his head either to steady her shaking legs or to try and guide him where she wanted him. Either way, he was taking his time.

"I want you to marry me as soon as possible. If you want to have a big wedding later; in fact, I'm sure between our two families they'll insist on it; but you're going to be my wife before then." He lifted the skirt up to her panties. "I'm going to drink from you, love. Taste you until you come in my mouth."

"Please," she begged him. "I can't take much more of this, Michael. You're killing me."

Sliding her panties from her wet sheath, he fit his finger inside of her. She shuddered against him, rocked hard onto his hand. Her fingers tightened in his hair. He knew the moment she started to come; her eyes fluttered closed and she trembled around him. Taking her pussy into his mouth, Michael drank.

She was sweet and spicy, warm and liquid. He moved his free hand to her ass and cupped her tighter to him. He felt her wetness running down his chin; her body convulsed around him and his cock leapt to take her. Reaching down to his fly, he undid his snap and eased his zipper down over his aching cock. He could feel his own pre-cum as he stroked it. When she came a third, then a fourth time, he gently laid her back on the bed and stood.

"Christ, you're beautiful. I could easily spend my entire life looking at you." His cock pulsed in his hand when she licked her lips. "I'm going to strip down, then I want you to do the same.

Slowly, so that I can imagine what you're going to take off next, what you're going to show me."

Michael peeled off his pants and his boxers at the same time. It wasn't that he was trying to rush, but he was afraid if he tried to remove them one at a time he'd killed himself. When he stood before her naked he reached for his cock again and began to fist it. He was very close to coming, but desperately wanted to be buried deep within her first.

Telling her to stand, he pulled her into his arms and kissed her. He did try to be gentle, but she tasted like sex and he wanted a full meal. When he finally pulled back they were both panting. He rocked into her softness.

"Michael, I know that you want to take this slowly, but if you don't take me now I'm going to resort to raping you." She reached for his cock and the simple brush of her hand nearly sent him over the edge.

"Lie down. And don't touch me. I promise you, I'll take you, but please let me do this my way." She nodded, but he wasn't sure about the look in her eyes. "I love you."

She laid down on the bed and he crawled up her body. When he was holding himself over her he looked down into her eyes. She looked hungry and he was ready to feed her.

He fisted his cock again and, while he watched her face, slowly entered her. She was slick and hot, her sheath tight and made for him. When he was nearly buried to the hilt, he settled himself over her body and raised her hands above her head with his own. She rocked up into him as he bore down into her welcoming heat.

"Michael, oh God, yes," she screamed as she came. Lacing his fingers with hers he rocked slowly, watching her face for every nuance, every flicker of her lashes. Michael thought that he loved her before, but when she looked up at him and screamed out his name again and again he tumbled so far and so fast that he knew he'd found his home.

As she came again, he let himself go, filled her with his seed. He continued to rock deep within her even after he was spent. When he finally collapsed on top of her he closed his eyes and rolled to his back, taking her with him.

He was nearly asleep when she said his name. He stirred but didn't move, answering her with a small sound. He smiled when she spoke with a yawn in her voice.

"I've been off the pill since I was taken. If this didn't get me pregnant, would you mind much if we tried again tomorrow, just to be sure?" She yawned again. "I think we should practice this all the time."

"Whatever you want, love. Whenever you need me."

Chapter 25

"I don't care, just fucking make it stop hurting. Damn it, you said that you'd help me when this time came. If you think this is helping me, then you're fucking off your rocker."

Cain looked down at his sister then over at her husband. He had to laugh. Poor Michael looked ready to run from the room. He didn't blame him, he was a little surprised by the venom in Gracie's voice too. He nearly said something to calm her when she grabbed his arm.

"Damn it, Gracie, that hurt. I told you that you needed to get her when the contractions started not when you were almost ready to deliver. Now there isn't any time for an epidural." He stepped back before she could touch him again. "You'll be fine. Women have been giving birth for centuries and—"

"I don't give a good flying fuck about anyone else right now. And I couldn't leave earlier. Trace had a football game tonight and I couldn't miss it. His team is going—fuck that hurts." Michael paled again.

Cain looked at the monitor and smiled. She was peaking every two minutes now. It wouldn't be long before she'd be able to push. He wondered what they were going to say when the baby was born. Or babies, in this case. Cain thought about all the babies now that were in his family.

Quinn and Drew had five children, a set of triples and a set of twins. They decided that enough was enough and five was the limit. He wondered how long that would last and thought by this time in a couple of years, she'd be pregnant again.

Jazzie and Nathan had two. Both single births and both boys. They were beautiful and every bit as rambunctious as their mother. She took them with her on every book signing. She claimed they were the reason her sales were through the roof. The movie was going to be released in one week.

Lilliane and Shamus had one with another on the way. Cain was happy for them both and when Shamus told him that they were expecting again, he looked like he might have invented procreation. Cain didn't think Shamus' feet had touched the floor since he'd found out. They would soon have three after their own set of twins.

Sin and Payton had five children. They had adopted another infant after Tonya had started walking and had been taking in older children since. The last child, Charlie, had been a problem boy since his mother had dropped him off at the police station one day and never returned. He'd been with Sin and Payton for a little over a month and seemed to be coming along just fine. Cain secretly thought he was afraid of Sin, but didn't blame him. Cain was a tad afraid of her himself.

He and Alyssa had three children. Connor now had a pair of identical twin sisters. He loved them so much Alyssa had had to put him in preschool twice a week so she could spend time with them. Connor was very protective of his sisters.

And now Gracie Anne was having a baby. He looked at the monitor again and realized that she was having contractions about every minute. *Soon now*, he thought. *Soon.*

"All right, Grace, let's get this show on the road," Donald Paschal said. He was her doctor, as Cain couldn't...well, he didn't want to deliver his own niece and nephew.

"What the hell do you think I've been doing, dork-ass? Playing with myself?"

Michael burst out laughing and earned a glare from his wife.

"Ah, love, you do have a way with words when you're trying to meet a deadline." Michael kissed her full on the mouth. "Come on, let us show this good man how we put something together. When he says push, you push. And if you're a good girl and do it in less than five pushes, I'll take you to Paris for Christmas this year."

"I hate you, you know that, right? I don't want to go to Paris. I want you to get this monster out of me. And if you think I'm having another one, well you can just get that thing cut off. You're not touching me again."

Eight really good pushes later and both babies were born. The little boy came first and was named Derrick James, and the little girl was named Kimberly Guinnie. Both were very healthy and had all their fingers and toes. Cain went to the lobby to tell all the families. The cheering could be heard all over the floor.

~~~

Trace looked down at his brother. He certainly didn't look like he'd ever be able to play with him. He glanced over at his sister, wondering if he'd be considered a sissy if he told somebody he wanted to hold her too. He was just trying to figure out the best way to ask when Sin sat down beside him and plopped Kim into his arms along with his brother.

"They're kinda ugly, aren't they?" she said to him.

He looked up at her to see if she was kidding.

"Of course it could be because they look like your dad and not Gracie."

He looked at the babies in his arms. He thought they both looked like wrinkled up old apples, but didn't think he should point that out. He hoped to goodness they got better looking as they grew into their skin. If not, he was going to spend a lot of his time defending them.

"Mom said that she and Dad were going to let me have one to keep. That I had to give the other one back." Trace looked up at Sin. "You think she was kidding?"

Sin laughed. "I'm sure if you tried to put one of them back she'd probably brain you. No, buddy, I'm pretty sure she was kidding." She touched Kim's cheek. "They are so beautiful, aren't they?"

He didn't answer. He was too busy watching his dad kiss his mom. They did that a lot and he was getting used to seeing them together. When they'd come back from their honeymoon, they'd told him they were going to be having a baby and he'd been a little scared.

Every day for three months the bigger his mom got, he kept expecting them to send him away. But they didn't and now he had a room of his own in a big house and his dad was home all the time. Mom, too, when she wasn't at a runway show, whatever that was.

He grinned when Mom started crying. He knew she wasn't upset or hurt, but happy. She smiled so beautifully when she did that and Trace was beginning to enjoy making her laugh on his own. He was very happy with his new family.

"Your grandma said to tell you to take a picture and send it to her. She said to tell you that she wished she could have been here, but Grandda is sick with the flu still."

Trace looked up at his dad as Sin slipped away.

"You like them?"

Trace grinned. "They're okay. They sort of look like Grandda when he takes off his shirt in the summer, don't they?" He knew it would make him laugh and he wasn't disappointed. His mom looked at him and winked. Trace felt his heart swell with love and pride.

"Sort of, now that you mention it. Though I think they have more hair."

Trace nodded and kissed his sister on the head. "Dad, when we get home, do you think I could possibly sleep in their room? I want to make sure there aren't any noises that'll wake them up and scare them."

His dad nodded then rubbed his hand over his head. "That'll be fine, son. I'm sure your mother will appreciate it."

Trace looked down at his newest family and grinned. He was going to have so much fun with these two and he couldn't wait until he could tell them all about their new family.

He kissed them both on the head again and went to the bed where his mom was. She didn't even stop talking to her brother, but pulled him up in the bed with her and hugged him. Trace thought there was nothing better than being hugged and hugged her right back. Life was suddenly good.

About the Author

I woke up one morning and decided to give play time to the people in my head who were keeping me awake. Little did I know that they would be so relentless and want their time right now! I wrote for the pure joy of it and to entertain my family and friends. But mostly it was to get more than an hour of sleep without a story playing out. Of course, the more I write, the more they want. So…well, as a result of sleepless days (I work through the night as a gun toting grandma – nope not a vigilantly but an armed security guard) I have lots of stories written.

Hello! My name is Kathi Barton and I'm an author. I have been married to my very best friend Sonny for at times seems several lifetimes – in a good way, honey. And together we have three wonderful children and then the ones we brought into the world - Paul and Dale Barton, Jason and Wendy Barton and Danielle and Ben Conklin. They have given us seven of the greatest treasures on Earth. They don't live at home seven days a week! No, seriously, seven grandchildren – Gavin, Spring, Ben, Trinity, Sarah, Kelly and Kian.

Follow Kathi on her blog: http://kathisbartonauthor.blogspot.com/

www.ingramcontent.com/pod-product-compliance
Lightning Source LLC
Chambersburg PA
CBHW020619180626
46810CB00007B/2851